— Loveline

SLIM
PICKINGS

GERRI LAPIN

PAN MACMILLAN

First published 1992 by Pan Macmillan Publishers Australia

This Lovelines edition published 1993 by
Pan Macmillan Children's Books
A division of Pan Macmillan Publishers Limited
Cavaye Place London SW10 9PG
and Basingstoke
Associated companies throughout the world

ISBN 0 330 33068 3

9 8 7 6 5 4 3 2 1

A CIP catalogue record for this book is available from
the British Library

This is a work of fiction. All characters and events in the story are
imaginary and any resemblance to any person living or dead is
purely coincidental.

Typeset by Trade Graphics
Printed by Cox & Wyman Ltd, Reading

Chapter 1

'Three large scoops of icecream. Peppermint, honeycrunch and strawberry, lying on a bed of chocolate cake surrounded by pillows of whipped cream...'

Soula giggled loudly. 'Honestly, Mia. You make that sundae sound like a dirty weekend.'

Ignoring her interruption, I said, 'This icecream has to be homemade.'

'Yuk! Peanut butter again.'

While she peered inside her sandwich, I continued work on my latest creation. 'Eggs, cream and sugar, plus whole fresh strawberries...'

Soula butted in. 'What about starting off with your Nonna's fresh gnocchi?'

I closed my eyes against her voice. '...covered in chopped nuts, marshmallows and maybe a sprinkling of hundreds and thousands. Then two wafers placed on either side like angel's wings...'

'Angel's wings? Mia Spanetti!' Soula's tone was accusing. 'I thought you were going on a fruit diet!'

My eyes flew open. 'I'll bet it's never occurred to you, Soula Angelopolous, that D.I.E.T. is just another four letter word?'

'Almost as bad as W.O.R.K.'

We grinned at each other. But while I really appreciated Soula's sense of humour, the truth was that no matter how hard we tried inventing new games, or creating luscious new desserts, it still didn't really make our lives any more exciting.

It'd be different, I told myself, if only we had a couple of nice guys to spend time with. Different if those two spunks, Guy Prescott and Gerard Moloney, would notice we were around...

'How about D.E.B.T?' Soula broke in. 'Like

what you owe me for that pie. You didn't really need that, did you?'

'Course I did. Got to keep up my strength.'

But as I tossed the last piece of pastry, which tasted like it'd been heated up once too often, into the bin, I felt fat and miserable. Humungous. So why had I pigged out once again? It wasn't as if I hadn't eaten heaps already.

But instead of just admitting it, I squinted up at the ceiling and repeated, 'A girl's got to keep up her strength.'

'Some strength!' Soula shrieked in exasperation. 'Four sausage rolls, a king-sized packet of chips plus a pie and sauce...'

As her voice never needs amplifiers, a couple of kids passing by giggled loudly. But don't get me wrong. Behind all that noise she's got a brain like a laser. Steering her through the canteen door, and away from curious ears, I said, 'At least I skipped the Mars Bar.'

'So? You'll probably go out and buy two king-sized Violet Crumbles instead.'

'You know I hate Violet Crumbles.'

'Big deal. What about Cherry Ripes, Tim

Tams...'

'I won't, I won't,' I protested before she could lay an even bigger guilt trip on me that I already had. Thankfully, before I could get into a total hate session with myself, the buzzer sounded for afternoon class. Shoving our way through the crowd, we headed for the lockers. Soula was a couple of steps in front when a familiar shape caught my eye.

My heart gave a sudden lurch, then righted itself.

'Hey!' I nudged her shoulder. 'I just thought of another four letter word. How about G.U.Y?'

Soula's eyes rolled. But she waited until we'd collected our books and settled into Room 27 before saying sarcastically, 'Since when did you start hating Guy?'

I groaned. 'I don't hate Guy. It's just that these days he hardly remembers my name. You'd never guess we used to sit in the same room in primary school. Let's face it, Guy Prescott is about as interested in me as...'

I was about to say Cameron Daddo, or maybe Jon Bon Jovi, or even Tom Selleck, when Mr

Hesketh, our English teacher, walked into the room and glared around.

'Mia Spanetti and Soula Angelopolous,' he announced — Mr Hesketh rarely bothers with saying 'Hello', 'were the only two people to finish this last assignment. I assume the rest of this class has a good excuse for not handing in their homework?'

'Goody-two-shoes!' someone called from the back. Relieved at the distraction, the entire class burst into laughter.

I blushed and turned towards the voice. Karinna Bell, our class stunner and my rival for Guy's attention was, as usual, sitting so close to him she was practically squatting on his knee.

What's more, dressed in her usual skimpy black jumper and leotards, she was showing off every skinny curve...

Karinna's such a snake, I told myself. I bet she sheds that gear twice a year. Just like a second skin...

Karinna guessed what I was thinking because, avoiding Mr Hesketh's sharp eye, she made a rude sign at me, mouthed 'fatty' and smiled. Out of the corner of my eye I watched Guy's mouth twitch...

Ignoring my insides, which were curling up with anger and embarrassment, I hissed at Karinna in my best Dracula voice, 'Watch it! We have ways off dealing with people like you.'

But Mr Hesketh had no intention of wasting valuable class time. He interrupted what might have been a thoroughly interesting exchange by telling everyone to open their books to page fifty-six.

While he droned on about the difficulties of handling Year 11 and the new VCE, plus the importance of getting assignments in on time, I tuned out for the rest of that lesson.

How come Guy was always around when something stupid was happening?

How come Guy was never around when things were going right?

No wonder Karinna was having a much better time than me. No wonder she had Guy Prescott almost, but thankfully not quite, under her long, red thumbnail.

You see, even though Soula and I are A-grade

students, even though everyone thinks we've got 'great personalities', who's going to date a girl whose figure reminds you of the Fat Lady in a circus?

But really, Soula and I aren't ugly. Soula's pretty stunning to look at. She has curly long black hair, creamy smooth skin, and big brown eyes. The corners of her mouth usually turn up in a smile, her teeth are a living ad for toothpaste and her body curves in and out in all the right places.

But it makes no difference. The guys at Donyvale Senior High, guys like Gerard Moloney and Guy Prescott for instance, won't see beyond those extra fifteen kilos she carries.

As for yours truly... Soula thinks I look pretty good too. So at least there's one other person in the whole world who thinks the other looks fine. Soula and I also have a whole lot of other things in common, but what holds us together — especially when life gets tough and the guys we're crazy about don't seem to know we're alive, is our mutual passion for food.

That's where our troubles begin and end. I

mean, sharing an enthusiasm for food would be okay if we both stuck to collecting cookbooks, and reading and cooking our favourite recipes. But what's the point of being able to prepare homemade fettucini with a rich Bolognaise sauce if you don't get to sample the results? And to make things worse, both of us have the kind of metabolism nature has designed to cope with a famine.

Soula reckons she could survive forever on just a lettuce leaf or maybe half a bowl of spinach. According to her, even when she barely eats at all she's still lucky to lose a gram.

For all I know she may be right. I really wouldn't know. The truth is, neither of us have ever tried starving, or living on a lettuce leaf for anything more than just a few hours.

So how come we're like this? Well, it's partly because of our families. Both Soula's and my folks have always had a passion for food as long as they can remember. Though Mr and Mrs Angelopolous recently got divorced, Mr Angelopolous imports various kinds of expensive olive oils and cheese. Soula's mum used to work with him, but when she and Mr Angelopolous split, she opened a takeaway specialising in delicious homemade pies and sandwiches.

As for us, Dad trained as a chef in Italy. He migrated to Australia sixteen years ago, just before I was born. Then, after years of working in other people's restaurants, he struck out on his own. But instead of starting up his own expensive bistro, he thought it was time Melbourne had a better standard of takeaway, and opened up a pizza parlour.

Because he's such a good chef, not to mention a hard worker, he quickly made it the best Pizzeria this side of the City. These days he specialises in his twenty-six different kinds of delicious crunchy toppings; he's an expert at baking the thinnest crispiest bases you've ever tasted and his pizzas are so famous, customers come from all over town to buy them.

It took Dad ages to get things started. As soon as the business took off, he needed more help. So rather than employ a stranger (who'd probably steal his recipes and set up in opposition), Mum left Nonna, my grandmother, to raise me and my twelve-year-old brother, Tony, and went to work with Dad.

I don't think Mum minded too much. Tolerant as she is, sharing the housekeeping with your mother-in-law, no matter how well you both get on, can be sheer murder.

Mum has an easy going personality. Whenever Dad or Nonna try and argue with her, she just smiles her special smile, like being nice to the family is the most natural thing in the world. She just kind of keeps on keeping on.

And as Nonna's pretty cool, at least as far as Italian grandmothers go, Mum's methods mostly work.

The only person who's got a problem is me.

You see, Nonna's always pushing something tasty into my hand. She can't bear seeing anyone she loves not eating. You don't have to be a psychologist to realise it's a result of her growing up in hard times, always having a terrible gnawing empty feeling in her stomach. If Nonna has any sort of dream it's that no one in her family should ever feel hunger again.

Anyway, while Tony, my little brother, can eat as much as he likes and stay lean as a lizard, it's different for me. Though I'm only one hundred and fifty two centimetres in my socks, if you go by those charts which tell you how many kilos you should weigh, there are twelve kilos which I'd give anything to be able to blink away. And if you multiply those kilos by two and half, that makes thirty-six pounds of excess fat.

P.S. Thinking over what I've just said, I suppose I shouldn't complain. Though it's Dad's fault I developed my love for food, I've also learnt to recognise a roulade, a quiche and a souffle. Dad says I should be considering a career in the hospitality business. I've promised him I'll think it over.

Chapter 2

The afternoon dragged on and on.

When the final buzzer sounded, I tore outside and casually positioned myself against the main steps. The idea was that when Guy came past, he might invite me to walk home with him.

Determined not to seem obvious, I half closed my eyes and pretended I was asleep.

My performance was so convincing, I woke up just in time to see Guy, together with Gerard Moloney and Mark Hibberd, all on their bicycles, disappearing down the street.

And then, rubbing salt into the wound, I caught sight of Karinna Bell being dinked home on the back of Guy's bike.

'It's hopeless,' I told Soula as we made our way to my place. 'I'm going to be miserable the rest of my life. It'll mar my personality for ever. One day I'm going to feel bad enough to jump in front of a train, or something. Maybe I'll even join a nunnery...' I visualised myself in a nun's habit, my hands folded in front of me in prayer, my face wan and holy looking...

To my surprise, instead of giggling like she usually does, Soula snapped, 'What a load of garbage!'

Soula usually listens to my moaning without flipping a hair. But today something must've been wrong, because as we were turning into my street, she snapped.

'All the time you've liked Guy, and I've been crazy about Gerard, we've never looked honestly at what interests them. Isn't it time we admitted that they only like a girl if she's got long legs, a small bum and big boobs?'

I stopped dead in my tracks. 'You've been

reading...'

Soula butted in. 'Anyway, what's so fantastic about Guy Prescott?'

'What do you mean by what's so terrific about Guy? You know anyone with such fantastic cheekbones, that beautiful jaw line, the way his blond hair flops into his eyes? I reckon he leaves Tom Cruise for dead.'

Soula stared at me, then giggled. 'I reckon Gerard's pretty gorgeous, too. The trouble is... neither of us look like Nicole Kidman...'

But I was pretending not to hear. 'What does Karinna Bell have that I haven't...?'

'You mean, what *hasn't* she got that you have?'

'Let's face it,' I muttered — sometimes other people's honesty really hurts — 'Neither Guy nor Gerard go for plump girls.'

Soula shrugged. We walked silently on. Then, in her usual practical way, pretending we hadn't already tried a million times in the past, she said, 'Last time we went on a fruit diet, we gave up right away. What about we have another go?'

'What diet are you talking about in particular?' I asked crossly. Poor Soula. I was being so cranky and she was only trying to help. 'I reckon we've tried just about every diet ever invented.'

'Have we ever.' She giggled. 'Remember the chocolate diet?'

'Uh-uh. But the idea behind it was terrific.'

'Yeah?' Her eyes rolled. 'Remind me, will you?'

'Same principle as working in a chocolate factory,' I said. 'The idea is, if you only eat heaps of one thing you'll eventually get sick of it, and you'll never face it again.'

'It was fun while it lasted.' Soula sighed.

'So why didn't it work?'

'Because we're hopeless chocoholics.'

I nodded slowly. 'Nothing,' I groaned, 'but nothing will ever make us hate Tim Tams and Jaffas.'

'Cherry Ripes and Mars Bars...'

'Smarties and devil's food cake...'

By now the corners of Soula's mouth, and she usually has the happiest personality of anyone I know, including my mum, were pointing down.

'It was a terrible, terrible disaster,' she moaned. 'I put on five kilos in one week and had the worst zits ever.'

'Let's face it...' By now we'd reached my front door and I was searching in my pocket for the key, 'We've tried just about everything known to woman. We tried the fruit diet...'

'The grapefruit diet.'

'The no carbohydrate diet.'

'The counting kilojoule diet.'

'The macrobiotic diet.'

'Remember the Israeli army diet?'

'Do I ever?' I banged the front door shut. 'That was when we had to stick to two days of eating only one food.'

'Uh-huh. But in a certain order: two days of apples, two days of salad, two of chicken and two of cheese.' She hung her jacket on the coat rack and dumped her bag underneath.

'And it really worked. I lost two kilos in a week.'

I hung my things next to her's. 'But you put three back on in the next.'

Soula nodded thoughtfully. 'Then Karinna Bell said cigarettes curbed her appetite so we took up smoking and spent all our money on Alpines...'

'Well, that didn't work either. All those ciggies ever did was give you a bad cough and make me throw up. Then I was hungrier than ever...'

But Soula wasn't listening. Something marvellous was drifting towards us. Nonna was in the kitchen and, judging by the smells, cooking the evening meal.

Our noses leading us down the corridor, we opened the kitchen door.

Nonna's face lit up.

'*Come stai*, Nonna?' I bent over to kiss her cheek. Nonna's wrinkled skin is as soft as the petals of a rose and as brown as a nut. Her hair is streaked with grey, her eyes are like little black olives, and her sturdy body is shaped exactly like an avocado.

'*Bene, bene,*' she muttered in Italian. 'You little horror. Why did you leave your room in such a mess?'

I ignored the question long enough to ask, '*Nonna, cosa cucini per stasera?*' (Nonna, what are you cooking?) and peered into her saucepans.

A quick rap across the knuckles. '*Qualco spa di buono.*' (Something good).

With this Nonna went back to watching her frypan. Because she's never got around to learning much English, she hardly ever speaks unless she has something important to say, and then rarely to anyone but a member of the family. I guess the amazing thing is how she manages to run the house, do the shopping and the cooking, all with her mouth firmly closed.

I looked around to see Soula hungrily eyeing the pile of crisp schnitzels Nonna had carefully arranged on a warming plate.

'Maybe we should get around to keeping track of what we eat,' I said, watching Soula's famished expression, 'Keep count of every single calorie and kilojoule. Write it all down.'

Soula grimaced. 'Four hundred and twenty eight calories in four grams of schnitzel,' she reminded me — Soula has an amazing memory for certain unpleasant facts. 'Multiply that by four and a half and you have the kilojoule count. Scary, isn't it?'

Stunned into total silence, I just nodded. My brain might be telling me I didn't need anything to eat, but the gap in my stomach was sending a totally different message to the salivary glands in my mouth.

Sensing our hunger, Nonna covered a plate with a delicious, mouthwatering schnitzel, heaped a huge mound of pasta covered in her special tomato sauce on the side and said to me, 'Your mother rang to say she won't be home until late and you're to eat as soon as you get home.'

Her message delivered, she handed the plate to Soula.

Soula reached for a knife and fork and said, 'Let's start dieting tomorrow.'

Reaching for another plate filled to capacity with what I knew was the best dinner in town, I quickly agreed.

Chapter 3

Weird to think how one small shift in your daily routine can alter your whole life.

Soula and I are still amazed at how nothing might ever have changed, how we might have gone on moaning and groaning like before, if the next day after school we hadn't visited our local newsagency.

Instead of my usual copy of *Dolly* I picked up this week's edition of *Rita* and flicked through the pages.

Soula was immediately suspicious. 'What do

you need that for? We've got heaps of back copies. My mum used to buy *Rita* every week.'

I pointed to the cover. Across it was the photo of a woman, she was a young looking forty, around my mum's age, only a whole lot trimmer. The caption read:

Is your teenager overweight?

Here's something practical you can do to help before the rot sets in…

See page 27.

'You got any money?' I asked Soula.

She peered in her purse like she hadn't a clue. 'Not much!'

'So lend me five.'

She looked like she was going to refuse. Instead, handing over a five dollar note, she couldn't resist adding, 'Don't think I've forgotten you owe me eight dollars from last week, and a dollar fifty for yesterday's pie.'

I quickly nodded. Before she could change her mind, and without even bothering to turn to page twenty-seven and check what we were buying — I mean, I was getting pretty desperate, I quickly paid the lady behind the counter and we took *Rita* back to Soula's.

I read through the article very carefully. The last paragraph said, ...*if you allow your teenager to carry too much excess weight, that same teenager will, years later, be a major candidate for gallbladder problems, a high cholesterol count and maybe even bowel cancer.*

'Terrific!' said Soula after she finished. 'Is that what you spent my money finding out?'

'No!' I pointed to the bit that really interested me. A small advertisement on the right hand corner of the page:

Camp Avalon has developed a sensible and practical program which specialises in helping teenagers with eating problems.

Ring toll free number 008 123 567 for our brochure, Or write to Box 234 N.S.W.

'What do you reckon we check it out?'

Soula shrugged, and turned to page 138, which happened to be next month's Star Guide.

'Don't be taken in by unlikely promises,' she read aloud. 'Stick to what you know to be right, and in the long run things will start working out...'

'Jeez, Soula,' I cried. 'Don't be like that! It sounds great. When we were little we always liked sleeping out in tents.'

'Me like bugs and cold and dirt, and sleeping out in tents? Yuk! You've got to be kidding.' And before I had a chance to explain, she moaned, 'Have you forgotten the Year 11 camp at Wilson's Prom?'

'It'll be heaps better than that,' I promised, mentally crossing all my fingers and toes in case it wasn't.

'This time I promise it'll be better,' I said firmly. 'This time it'll be heaps better.'

'I'll bet!' Soula's smile was disbelieving. 'It's bound to cost heaps, and the place'd be full of fat, spoilt little brats. I can see them now...' she put on a husky voice. 'We don't eat this, and we only eat that...'

'Yeah,' I grinned. 'The place'll be full of fat little brats. Just like us.'

As I kept on grinning, she couldn't stop herself from laughing back. It crossed my mind how, when both of us were little and already best friends, we'd blow dandelions into the wind, and pray like mad that our wishes would come true. Back then, our wishes were simple; like we'd wish that our mums'd take us to the zoo or the cinema. Or maybe for a doll or a bike.

But now, watching Soula's wary expression, I suddenly felt sad. Why don't things ever stay the same? You see, when you're little, deep down somewhere you really believe your wishes will come true. I reckon growing up is realising they probably won't...

'Maybe you're right,' I sighed. 'Maybe they'll feed us on lettuce leaves and diet jelly and we'll nearly starve to death. But I'm going to ring and see what it's all about.'

Soula looked a bit alarmed. 'Send them a letter. Why don't you write?'

'Writing's too slow.'

'But it costs a fortune to ring! Look... a NSW number. Since Mum got the last Telecom bill, she's threatened to key the phone so I can never ring out without asking first.'

I waved the magazine in her face. 'You're being

pathetic. 008 means a toll free number. It costs the same as a local call.'

Soula still looked uncertain, so I picked up the phone and dialed. When a very matter-of-fact female voice said, 'This is Camp Avalon,' I knew I had the right place.

I told the voice on the other end that I was Mrs Spanetti and I wanted a copy of their brochure. When she asked for my address I gave her Soula's. I didn't want Nonna knowing too much about this latest venture. I know how her mind works. She'd only say that though I *was* a little plump, basically I was a perfect size. It wouldn't matter how much I argued. Even if I were to point out that there were heaps of reasons apart from weight control for me needing to go, she'd stop the conversation halfway by telling me I was carrying on like a spoilt kid. Then, before I could come up with any decent kind of answer, she'd just walk away.

The voice on the other end brought me back to the present by assuring me she'd make sure the brochure was in the mail as soon as possible. One way and another, the whole thing took about five seconds flat.

'That's that.' I put down the phone. 'Didn't hurt, did it?'

Soula still looked doubtful. When she went back to munching a Tim Tam, I changed the subject to the end of term social, and the clothes we had, or rather didn't have, to wear.

'What's the point of worrying?' Soula moaned. 'Whatever we wear we look fat and frumpy. No one'll notice us except Karinna, and she'll only make some nasty crack to make us look stupid. I can just see her, Joanne and Tara...'

'Don't tell me.' I half closed my eyes. 'They'll be in skin tight spangly numbers, hems up somewhere near their thighs, really high heels...'

All this time we'd been sitting on Soula's bed nibbling potato chips and Tim Tams, and sipping on a couple cans of Coke. Without any warning Soula hopped off, raced over to her wardrobe, which takes up one entire wall, flung the door open and pointed at the contents.

'Three kinds! Fat, fatter, and fattest!'

'Only three?' I laughed. 'I've got four. Fat, fatter, fattest and "Clothes for the Frankly

Obese".'

'You're missing the point. Even with all this,' Soula gestured dramatically, 'I haven't got anything to wear.'

'Me neither. We need to think of a way of getting our parents to shout us new gear.'

'What's the use?' For a moment Soula looked like she'd lost her last cent or been told she had a terminal illness. 'Dad'll give me the money. He feels so guilty about Mum and him splitting up and him never seeing me, he gives me anything I want. And we'll even go shopping. But you know the problem...there's never anything decent to buy.'

There was no arguing with that. You see, while most people think a licence to shop is a dream come true, for Soula and me, buying clothes is basically a nightmare. Most of our clothes consist of ordinary jeans, huge skirts, jackets and flowing shirts which tie together somewhere under the hips. We work on the principle of covering up as much as possible. Every magazine article I've ever read which discusses *What big girls ought to wear*, emphasises loose clothes, dark colours and chunky jewellery. I've got quite a collection of interesting rings, earrings and scarves. But when it comes to glamour, or anything far out, I just shut my eyes and wish myself far away. I mean, look at what happened the last time I went hunting for a decent pair of bathers?

Soula must've dragged me to just about every store in town, but the only bathers made in a size sixteen were in the departments labelled BIG SIZES. What's more, they were mostly plain black and had built in bras and little skirts draped across their fronts which hid the tops of your thighs.

But the worst thing of all are the dressing-rooms. Every dressingroom I've ever come across has a set of brightly lit full length mirrors arranged so you can see yourself from every angle and sap all your confidence. I'm not exactly sure how Soula feels about checking out her appearance because she'll never, ever admit to feeling that bad, but as for me... looking at all that flesh hanging out is the most depressing sight in the whole wide world.

I wasn't always fat. I can still remember, when

I was about three or four, Nonna forcing me to finish all my meal, even spanking me if I said I wasn't hungry. And somehow or other, it's become so deeply ingrained that I just can't do anything about it. If I don't eat everything on my plate, even ask for more, I'm a really bad girl.

It's not as if it's just me who enjoys pigging out. I mean, all we Spanettis love food. What's more, we love everything to do with food. We love reading recipes, planning dishes, working out lists and shopping for the ingredients. Our bookshelves are filled with the best collection of recipe books you're ever seen; everything from Mrs Beeton to Vogue Gourmet, and our pantry and king-sized fridge and freezer just about groan with delicious bits and pieces.

A great day's outing for us is going to the markets to bargain with the stall- holders, choosing just the right meat, fruit, vegies, cream, cheese and salamis to make a particular dish. We would never dream of having any sort of family celebration that didn't involve all of us attending a really good restaurant. But what we mostly love is sitting around our own diningroom table with maybe a few friends, talking and eating.

And except for my little brother Tony, who, no matter how much he eats always stays skinny, the others don't mind being plump. Nonna thinks bigger is best, and Dad is a real advertisement for his own food. And though Mum talks heaps about wanting to lose weight, Dad says he likes her as round and soft as a butterball. The real problem is me. You see, while almost everyone I know expects a girl to behave like she really hates food, even look a teensy bit anorexic before they think she's okay, Nonna and Dad keep pressing me to eat.

Whenever Soula feels really bad about the way she looks, I tell her it's not as if people have always been like this. I mean, there's heaps of evidence to prove that earlier this century, people really worked at staying plump. I've seen photos of Clara Bow who was a star of silent movies, and of Mae West. By today's standards both of them were pretty fat. And look at Marilyn Monroe. Though she was skinnier than me, she had decent sized thighs and breasts, and a tummy that was definitely concave instead of convex.

There's heaps of other cultures, too, who like their women large. Take the Arabs or Indians for instance. According to Dad, in India only the very poor are thin. He once told me that if you pick up a Pakistani newspaper or magazine, or see an Indian film, all the models and actresses are very well rounded.

Still, while mentioning all this makes me feel heaps better, it doesn't help Soula and me find some decent clothes for next week's dance, does it?

Chapter 4

Two days later Soula phoned me to talk about Gerard.

Personally, though I've never liked Gerard very much, I feel like I've known him forever. You see, all five of us — Guy, Gerard, Karinna, Soula and yours truly — went to the same primary school down the road. And even though we didn't see each other for a while after we left because Karinna, the guys, Soula and me, all went to different Junior Highs, this year we met up again in Year 11 at Donyvale Senior.

The weird thing is that back in primary school,

the five of us were best friends. We used to
call our gang The Overlookers, mainly because
a teacher once accused us of 'over-looking'
what everybody else was doing. But where you
might've thought those four intervening years
shouldn't make too much difference to really
good mates, even though we didn't see each
other too often, those years changed things
between us a lot.

For one thing, Karinna stopped acting like
a friend and became really competitive. And
while we would have liked the guys to stop
treating us as mates, they kept on doing it, only
more so…much more so. Guy never misuses his
friendship, but I reckon Gerard takes advantage
of Soula's good nature. I mean, he's always
borrowing her assignments, copying them out
with maybe a couple of minor changes, then
passing them in as his own. Yet when it comes
to taking Soula out, even to just buying her
a cappuccino and a piece of cheesecake, he'll
pretend they've never met.

But for some peculiar reason, Soula competely
ignores his scummy behaviour. Pretends it isn't

happening. What's worse, she's convinced that Gerard is going to ask her to the Year 11 social.

'I reckon he's interested,' she keeps assuring me. 'It's just that he's shy.'

Even with someone as close to me as Soula, sometimes it's hard being tactful. 'But isn't he keen on Tara?' I said cautiously. 'I mean, like they're always together, aren't they?'

'He acts like he's keen on Tara,' she admitted, but I could tell from her quavery voice she was trying not to face facts. I mean, except for Soula, everyone in Year 11 knows Tara and Gerard are going together.

After she rang me that night to talk some more about Gerard, she eventually got around to mentioning that the Camp Avalon brochure had arrived.

My ears pricked up. 'What's it like?'

'Looks like a take...' I managed to decipher through whatever she was chewing.

I shifted the phone to my other ear. 'Yeah? What does it say?'

'Mmm.' There was more sounds of chewing, the rustle of paper and a long, long silence.

Then, 'They've got all these exercise programs and things.'

I groaned to myself. 'When's it being held?'

'Straight after Christmas. Up near Warburton. They rent a big boarding house with good sporting facilities.'

'Well, at least it's not camping out in tents.'

'Lettuce leaves and diet jelly,' Soula snapped. Suddenly her voice was very clear.

Something more important was bothering me. Ignoring her crabby tone, I asked, 'How much does it cost?'

'What do you reckon? Heaps.'

My heart sank. 'How do you mean, heaps?'

She named an astronomical figure, then giggled loudly.

'Nine hundred and fifty dollars for two weeks?' I shrieked. 'I don't believe it.'

'So that ends that, right?'

'Right,' I said doubtfully.

Maybe if Soula hadn't sounded so pleased, I might've agreed. But something in her voice, maybe the quick way she went back to talking about Gerard and Guy, made me dig in my heels.

'Don't forget to bring that brochure to school tomorrow,' I ordered.

'Sure, sure...'

'I really want to read it.'

'I told you I would, didn't I?'

I still wasn't convinced, but I let it go at that.

The next day in geography, Mrs Wilson, our usual teacher was away. Mr Hesketh poked his balding head and shaggy beard through the door.

'If you've finished your assignment on Australian deserts,' he said, 'catch up on some reading.'

Though my assignment still had a long way to go, I took his advice and caught up on some important reading of my own.

The Camp Avalon brochure was glossy and expensive. You could almost see the dollar signs dripping from the envelope. The cover showed a boy and girl who could've been twins. Both were blond, tall and slim, and both were dressed in identical blue track suits with the CAMP AVALON logo across the front.

I turned to the first page.

'According to this,' I said to Soula, who was working away like a beaver, 'the camp has only two to a room and every couple of rooms shares a bathroom. Sounds great!'

'Yeah?' Soula didn't look rapt. 'Guess it depends on who's doing the sharing.'

'I wouldn't go unless we shared,' I promised.

She still didn't look impressed.

The next few pages were filled with photos: Shots of slim, suntanned, healthy looking people splashing around in the pool, playing basketball, billiards, doing aerobics, canoeing, sitting at a diningtable eating, even picnicking around a camp fire.

I turned to the second last page;

It's the careful combination of diet and exercise, I read aloud, *'which gives Camp Avalon its amazing results. Your teenager is guaranteed to learn healthier living and eating habits. Each teenager will have a special diet and exercise program especially tailor made for him or her. All this will be under the care of a specialist instructor...*

'Forget it, Mia,' Soula interrupted. 'I showed Mum that brochure. She says it's a great idea, but we can't afford nine hundred and fifty bucks.'

'Oh.' I thought for a moment. 'What about your dad? He'll give you anything you ask for.'

She shook her head. 'Nothing doing. Business is crook. Since the recession, no one's buying imported oils and cheeses. There's no way I can get nine hundred and fifty together by Christmas.'

She sounded so definite, there was nothing I could say, or do, to make her change her mind.

Come to think of it, lately Mum and Dad weren't looking too happy. And the other day, when I'd asked Mum if I could buy some new clothes for this week's social, she got really upset. And it occurred to me that maybe they were finding things hard too.

'Of course...' I was thinking out loud, 'We can always earn the money ourselves.'

Soula's laugh was so loud everyone stopped whatever they were doing to stare at us. Once things settled down, she whispered fiercely, 'Wake up Australia. Don't you know things are tough out there? Ten percent of people are out of work.'

What a wimp! And before we even got started!

'Sometimes, Soula,' I practically snarled, 'you're just so defeatist, I can't believe it.'

'Defeatist, smefeatist. There aren't any jobs.' And she went back to her assignment.

'But there's got to be *something!*' I insisted.

Soula put down her pen and turned round to face me. 'Like what?'

As I couldn't think of an answer, at least not right away, I said, 'I'll think of something. You wait and see.'

Popping the Camp Avalon brochure back into its envelope, I picked up my geography assignment and got stuck right in.

Chapter 5

For Soula and me the Year 11 social was a complete disaster. Being perfectly honest, even more of a wash-out than the Year 11 camp.

Lunchtime the day of the dance, the other members of the Social Committee got together to decorate the school hall with balloons and streamers. And even if I say so myself, the end results were terrific. Everyone was expecting a really great night.The committee had hired a great DJ, paid a couple of the bigger Year 12 guys to keep unwelcome visitors away, and persuaded everyone in Year 11 to put in ten dollars each so we could get some really good food and drink.

This last idea was mostly mine. As most school functions never seem to have anything more exciting to eat than frozen party pies, or soggy sandwiches and stale potato chips, I'd already asked Mr Hesketh to give Soula and me permission to skip class and spend the day cooking. Though it was my idea to do the supper, it was definitely Soula's decision to make the night an international one. We'd spent most of the previous week planning the menu and writing lists. The morning of the social we went shopping for the ingredients. Mrs Wilson, our Home Economics teacher, let us use her kitchen...specially after we faithfully promised we'd leave it in the same condition as we found it.

Anyway, cutting a long story short, it took us most of the day to cook and fill several large casserole dishes with Italian lasagne, and half a dozen egg and bacon pies lined with my special homemade shortcrust pastry... soon as it hits your mouth it melts away to almost nothing.

Meanwhile Soula prepared Greek moussaka and Indonesian sate chicken, and we both got together to produce a huge mound of Chinese fried rice and three bowls of French salad.

For dessert we'd already baked two cheesecakes with whole strawberries on top, prepared three trays of chocolate fudge brownies, two large bowls of port wine trifle and two huge lemon meringue pies.

To prepare so much food was a huge effort, but when we stood back to see what we had accomplished, everything looked absolutely mouthwatering. Even Mrs Wilson — and she's usually really fussy about how a meal is planned and presented, said we'd cooked everything to perfection.

So perhaps it was because we were dead tired by the end of that day, or maybe because we tasted more than we should've, only what could've been a great night turned into the biggest fizzer ever.

Our first problem was that neither Soula nor I could afford anything special, or new, to wear.

Nonna had offered to fix up my favourite black

dress... let it out around the bust and hips so it wasn't so tight, and take up the hem. Then, after she'd put so much time and effort into the renovations, when I tried on the dress, it was a complete and total wash-out.

We both stared at my reflection. At last Nonna said, in Italian, 'Maybe your red jacket will hide where the zip won't do up.'

'But everyone'll guess the dress doesn't fit,' I wailed in English. Then burst into tears. 'Anyway, I'll be too hot in a jacket.'

'I could put in some extra material here.' Nonna pointed to where the waist refused to come together.

'Forget it.' I pulled the dress back over my head. There was a terrible ripping sound as the zipper finally gave way.

Poor Nonna. After all that work I must've seemed so ungrateful. But she must've realised how terrible I was feeling, because she tiptoed out of the room, taking the ripped dress with her.

I searched through my clothes, trying on everything I owned. Nothing fitted... not even in the 'Clothes for the Frankly Obese'. Then I went through Mum's wardrobe. Nothing fitted either. These last few months I must've put on more weight than I'd realised, because the only things which looked half decent were my largest pair of jeans, the ones I wore to school just about every day, and an outsized shirt which hung over my stomach and hips like a bright red flag. Catching sight of myself in the mirror, I decided maybe I could rent my body out as an auction sign. Or a warning for ROAD WORKS AHEAD.

Okay, my hair looked good, and my face, even if it was as round as a pudding bowl, was clear of zits. But did I look exciting, glamorous or romantic? Yuk! You'd have to be kidding.

Promptly at eight, Soula and her mum turned up to drive me to Donyvale. Soula was in a deep pink taffeta number which really suited her dark colouring, and her hair hung down in ringlets. I thought she looked pretty terrific, and I told her so, but all she could mutter was, 'This dress is so tight I can hardly breathe.'

Donyvale all lit up at night looked different enough for us to forget this was the place we attended every day of the week. So I did try to get into the spirit of things, I really did try. The real trouble began about an hour after the disco got started. What actually happened was this:

Soula and I had been dancing opposite each other when I noticed, out of the corner of my eye, Guy moving in my general direction. I kind of signalled to Soula what was happening, then casually danced his way.

Suddenly the best thing happened. Looking straight at me, he smiled into my eyes...

My heart did such a gigantic flip I was sure everyone must've noticed it pounding away in my chest. As we moved closer together, I stared at Guy's straight blond hair and aquamarine eyes, his high cheekbones and square chin with the dimple in the centre, those long lean legs and slim hips...

Suddenly I was on cloud nine. All my dreams were coming true. I could hardly believe it. Guy was rapt. He was rapt in me. He was mouthing something wonderful. He was telling me how much he really liked me.

I danced in closer to hear...

'Mia, I snuck a look at the supper,' he was

saying. 'You're such a fabulous cook. That supper's amazing. Right over the top. The best food I've seen in ages.'

My poor heart plummeted to my feet. A shove from the rear almost sent the rest of me flying.

What was going on?

I spun around. Karinna was dancing behind me. Her hands and feet moving independently, she was closing in on Guy. And I was left standing in the middle of the floor like the great goof I was, feeling completely worthless. All Guy cared about was my lasagna!

I rushed to the loo, locked myself in a cubicle, and cried until I felt sick. But once I calmed down a bit I peered at myself in the mirror. Was I really that hopeless?

I looked at my reflection carefully. My main negative, I decided, was that my face was so fat my eyes and cheekbones kind of got lost in roly poly folds.

But didn't I have a few positives too? Like my hair was naturally curly and its reddish tint had nothing to do with dye. And my eyes, which are a nice hazel with golden flecks are, except when I've been crying, usually okay. In fact Dad's always said their colour reminded him of a tiger. All the same, I thought, they'd look heaps better if they weren't hidden inside cheeks that reminded me of butterballs, oranges, pumpkins...

Then there's my nose. Unlike Karinna's, which tilts to one side like it's been hit by a cricket ball, it's straight, not too big or too small. My mouth is a normal kind of mouth, and my teeth are white and straight. My skin's another positive. I mean, unlike some other kids I know, I hardly ever get blackheads or zits.

But even while I told myself this, another little voice kept whispering, 'You're just avoiding the truth. Your real problem is that deep down somewhere, you can't imagine yourself any other shape...' Maybe, I thought, maybe if I made a huge, a humungous effort to lose some weight, maybe if I lost just a few kilos, I'd feel less like a wallflower. Then maybe Guy would stop seeing me as a terrific cook and more as a fabulous spunk.

So I stalked back into the hall and straight

over to where Soula was standing by the wall, watching Gerard dance with Tara.

'I've made up my mind,' I shouted in her ear. 'We're going to Camp Avalon.'

'What?' she shouted back.

'I've made up my mind,' I shrieked. 'The two of us are going to Camp Avalon — and nothing's going to stop us!'

Just then, the music ended and my voice boomed out above the crowd. Everyone stared, but I didn't care. For once I was determined. Soula and me were going to get thin, lose heaps of weight, look right, become known as spunks...

Or die trying!

Chapter 6

Making up your mind is one thing, doing something about it is another.

'Okay, so there aren't any jobs,' I said to Soula. 'We can always do things. Show a bit of initiative. Where's your entrepreneurial spirit?'

'Do things,' she repeated blankly. 'Things like what?'

'Well...' I thought quickly. 'What about washing cars? You draw up a sign, and I'll nail it to your fence.'

'Hmmnnn... that's one way to go.' Grabbing a sheet of paper, she started working out figures.

'What do we charge per car?'

I closed my eyes and thought. 'For just a wash, five dollars. A full clean, both inside and out, ten dollars. And for the whole deal; you know, inside and out and polishing up the duco, fifteen.'

When I opened my eyes, we got down to business.

Halfway through our calculations I realised that neither of us had a clue about how much car shampoo and polish cost. That meant a trip to the local supermarket. Then back home to work out heaps more figures.

When we finished, Soula stared at me in dismay. 'I never realised it all cost so much. We need a thousand cars to raise enough cash.' The corners of her mouth drooped. 'Where are we going to find a thousand dirty cars?'

I wasn't sure either, but then I had a new, even more inspirational idea. 'Forget the cars,' I said tearing open a fresh packet of Tim Tams. Helping myself to a couple, I passed the packet on to her. 'Holidays next week. Right? How about we spend some time washing windscreens at the train crossing?'

Soula looked horrified. 'Isn't that dangerous? What if a car comes racing through, doesn't see us and knocks us flying?' Reaching for a half finishéd packet of chocolate Teddy Bears, her favourite chocolate biscuit, she ignored the Tim Tams. Well, at least for the time being.

'Not if you're careful. There's a double set of red lights and the rail crossing gates. Providing we stay off the road when the lights turn green, we'll be fine.'

She nodded slowly. 'Right!' And through a mouthful of crumbs, 'What do we charge?'

'People can be very generous. Why don't we take whatever they give? I reckon that'll earn us heaps more than if we set a limit.'

'Uh-huh,' she said, but she still looked uncertain.

First thing Monday we got started. I'd already spent most of Saturday afternoon and Sunday morning checking the whole thing through. The idea was to wait for the traffic lights to turn red and the gates to close. By the time the train passed through and the gates reopened, seven minutes would have passed. And if two trains were racing through in opposite directions, that gave us ten whole minutes.

The way I figured it was this: as soon as the cars braked, we'd race in front of the driver swirling a bucket of warm soapy water in one hand and a squigee in the other.

A splosh of water on the windscreen, a quick rub down with the brush, first one side, then round the front of the car to the other, scraping the squigee against the glass to wipe away the soapy mess. Then, after just a few minutes, we'd have a spotless windscreen and be holding out our hands for the money.

Using Mum's car as our model, we timed everything. The average windscreen took me less than two minutes to wash and wipe free of soap and water. If we assumed that it would take the driver at least another minute to collect his loose change and pass it through the window, we would manage four cars each, every time a train passed through.

While we were busy experimenting on Mum's car, Dad came out to see what we were doing. He stared at us, the car, the bucket of soapy water and the squigee in disbelief.

'Why are you only cleaning the windscreen?' he demanded. 'What about the rest of the car?'

I grinned at him, and explained what we were doing. For one nasty moment, I thought he was about to blow his top. Then, to my surprise, he burst out laughing. 'What are you going to do if you wash their car and they don't pay?'

'They wouldn't dare!' Soula said.

Dad shook his head. 'Business is bad,' he pointed out. 'These days people's hands stick in their pockets. It's hard getting them out.'

'We'll just have to take the risk,' I said.

Dad nodded. 'Don't let them try any funny stuff,' he reminded us. With this he nodded again, and went straight back inside.

We went on planning our new business.

Next morning we were at the railway crossing in time to catch the peak of the rush hour.

I soon discovered my calculations had been a bit wrong. You see, it took us far more than an average of two minutes to get from one car to another. The basic problem was that most people took ages and ages to dig into their pockets and purses. Often we'd be left standing there with our hands held out, the lights would change, and we'd have to duck out of the way and onto the traffic islands before we were knocked over in the rush.

After the first hour was up, and the traffic had slowed down to a trickle, Soula and I met in the McDonald's down the road. As we were really hungry, I ordered two quarter pounders, two cheeseburgers, four packets of chips, two apple slices and two chocolate malteds, paying for them out of our profits.

I took them back to Soula who was lying half slumped over a table. 'Breakfast,' I announced.

She looked half dead already.

'For every ten windscreens,' she moaned, 'about three of them don't get around to paying. A couple of those guys got really abusive.' In spite of her exhausted state, she managed a half grin. 'I nearly asked one of them to open his window so I could take a swipe at his nose.'

I nodded tiredly. 'We're doing something stupid. Maybe it'd be easier if we tackled them together? You know, maybe one should handle the squigee while the other works on the cash?'

She stopped gulping down her breakfast long enough to say, 'Bags I get to collect.'

'Uh-uh.' I shook my head. She looked like she was about to argue, so I quickly said, 'We'll both take turns!'

Even so, by the time we'd taken the morning coffee break, then lunch and tea at McDonalds, we only managed to collect forty dollars between us.

The next day might've been better. I mean, we'd got much faster and more efficient, only the weather turned gruesome.

It drizzled all day. Not enough to make us go home, just enough to have every windscreen wiper in Melbourne flash backwards and forwards, and make our job useless.

After that we didn't bother going out if it looked at all like rain. And, just our luck, that fortnight was one of the wettest in years. Of our fourteen days holiday, it rained non-stop for ten.

The day before the start of term three, I invited Soula over for lunch. Mum and Dad have always made a point of keeping the shop closed for Sunday lunch so, according to Mum, 'We can eat together like a family should.' During the rest of the week we mostly snack in the kitchen, but Mum and Nonna always serve the Sunday meal in the dining-room.

After, as we sat round digesting Nonna's special Risotta and her super-duper chocolate cheesecake, Dad wanted to know how much the two of us had made?

'Altogether?' I glanced at Soula who rolled her eyes and refused to answer. 'One hundred and thirty five dollars and sixty two cents precisely.'

'After all that work?' Mum looked concerned. 'Is that all? I'm sorry about the money, darlings. We would have loved to pay for that camp, only things being as they are...' she glanced apprehensively at Dad, 'At the moment we can't meet some of our bills...'

The more she talked, the worse I got to feeling. After a while I interrupted her,

'I never expected you to hand me the cash. Anyway,' I added, 'We've heaps more time before the first payment's due.'

But later with Soula, in the privacy of my bedroom, I wasn't so optimistic. 'If we don't suddenly find a big lump of money soon,' I moaned, 'we'll never get to camp.'

She stared back. 'Like you said, we don't need *all* of the money until November. Maybe something'll turn up by then?'

'Like what?'

She was too busy chomping through a Mars Bar to answer. 'At the rate we're going,' she licked her lips free of chocolate, 'it'll take us three years to collect nineteen hundred dollars.'

'Probably heaps longer than that.'

Soula's voice got louder. 'I reckon I'll commit suicide if Gerard doesn't look at me soon.'

'Me too,' I said. Soula nodded. She knew I didn't mean Gerard. She knew exactly what I meant.

Someone up there must've heard us, because our big break came first thing next day.

Like always, Soula and I walked to school together. Just as we were rounding Patterson Street, and Soula was being boring about the thirty dollars she reckoned I owed her, I heard someone pounding up behind us. 'Hang on there, I want to talk with you.'

Karinna Bell, dressed in a trendy tracksuit and joggers, all sweaty and flushed from her run, fell into step beside us. 'You two interested in earning some money?'

How come Karinna knew? Soula glared at her suspiciously. 'You selling drugs or something?'

It didn't take us long to find out.

'Mum saw you washing windscreens at the railway crossing,' Karinna explained. Then she couldn't help saying, 'She said she'd never let me do anything so dangerous.'

'So? No one asked you, did they?'

'Anyway…' Karinna's eyes darted between us, but she had more important things on her mind than a possible fight, 'I told Mum about the great supper you did for the social. And she wants to know if you'll cater for my seventeenth birthday party?'

'Maybe,' I said cautiously. 'Depends on when it is.'

'Two weeks time. Mum hates cooking, but we

can't afford to hire proper caterers.'

Ignoring the reference to us not being 'proper caterers', I nodded. 'Depends on how many people you're having.'

'I've sent out fifty invitations.'

I thought for a moment. Fifty was quite a crowd to cook for. But hadn't we just done a supper for over seventy?

'How much you prepared to pay?'

Karinna's eyes narrowed. 'Mum says five bucks a head for food and drink.'

'Great!' And ignoring the grossness of Karinna not sending either Soula or me an invitation to her seventeenth birthday party, I burst out laughing.

Once I stopped I said, 'You don't need a caterer. Five bucks should just about cover three drinks each and a packet of potato chips.'

She glared at me. 'How much then?'

Hadn't the Year 11's paid ten dollars each and brought along their own drinks? And we hadn't had a cent left over. Besides, unless Soula and I made a decent kind of profit we'd never make it to Camp Avalon. Our problem was that the harder we tried raising that money, the more inaccessible those nineteen hundred dollars were becoming.

'Twenty-five dollars per person,' I said at last.

'Twenty-five dollars?' Karinna's voice rose. Even Soula looked shocked. 'You've got to be kidding. I'll pay twelve.'

'Fifteen dollars per person and you buy the drinks,' I said. I kept my voice firm but cool. Professional. And nothing Karinna, and later on Mrs Bell argued, or did, could make me back down.

Chapter 7

The morning after Karinna's seventeenth birthday party, Soula added up the figures — after opening a packet of chips.

'If I subtract what it cost us, we've made a clear profit of two hundred and fifty dollars.'

'Two hundred and fifty dollars,' I mused. 'Not bad for one night's work. So... how much have we got now?'

'You mean, including our savings and everthing?'

'Everything.'

She did a few more sums.

'Six hundred and thirty-eight dollars, and forty three cents.'

We stared at each other in dismay. 'Not even enough for one of us to go to Camp,' I groaned.

'After all that work and aggro.'

Soula opened a new packet of chips.

'Whoa,' I yelled, watching the chips disappear. 'What about sharing those?'

She absentmindedly handed them over. 'I meant to ask…what did Guy want to talk to you about?'

I emptied the rest of the packet into my mouth. 'Guess!'

'Can't!' Soula reached for the cashews. 'What did he say?'

'He and Gerard came over to tell me they thought the supper was terrific. Even better than the one we'd done for school. Guy thinks we should go into business.'

Soula's eyes rolled. 'What do you know. So what did you say?' She looked so cross, I couldn't help laughing.

'I reminded him that we *were* in business, and if

either of them hears of someone else who wants some catering done, they should let us know right away.'

The cashews halted in front of her lips. 'You reckon they will?'

'Gerard said he would. He knows someone who wants a twenty-first catered for.'

'You know something gross? Gerard wouldn't even talk to me. Once we got busy, I didn't see where he went.'

Gerard, I knew, had been with Tara.

I opened a fresh packet of chips.

'Guy spent the night with Karinna,' I mumbled at last, 'but Gerard went home early.'

While lying about Gerard was automatic, I thought maybe it was a big mistake. Was I really doing Soula a favour? Wouldn't it only hurt her more if someone else told her that Gerard had spent the night with Tara?

But there was no way *I* was going to tell her the truth. Quickly changing the subject, I said, 'Looks like we'll get more work soon. That's something to look forward to.'

'Yeah, something!'

We went back to chewing.

Gerard *did* contact his friend, who rang me two days later. In no time flat it seemed, the fame of our cooking had spread far and wide.

Catering for that guy's twenty-first birthday party was quickly followed by another. Then another. But we knew we'd really hit the big time when we were asked to provide a supper for a big engagement party. Over one hundred guests.

Though we'd never worked so hard in our lives, there was one unexpected result. You see, what with keeping up with Year 11 *and* running a business, there was never any time to get too upset over Guy and Gerard treating us more like aunts than potential girlfriends.

Not that either Soula or me ever lost sight of our goal. By November, when the first cheque had to be sent to cover our Camp Avalon booking, we had almost made enough money. Almost but not quite.

'We're still three hundred short of nineteen hundred dollars,' Soula told me over the phone. By now she was established as the finance half of the business, while I talked to the customers and helped plan their menus.

'And,' she added, 'in three days time the cheque has to be in the mail.'

'Only three days?' I paused. 'How much do we need?'

'The deposit? Five hundred dollars.'

'Haven't we got that much? Send them the money. We'll worry about the rest later on.'

'Ummm,' she said. Then, 'I don't think we should.'

'Why not?'

'If we don't come up with it all, we'll lose our deposit. I won't send anything until I'm dead sure we're covered.'

'If the worst comes to the worst,' I said hopefully, 'we can always borrow the rest. Ask your mum. Promise we'll pay it back soon as possible.'

Another, longer pause.

'I don't know about that. She's got some major expenses. Why not try yours?'

'No, better not. Tony's school fees are coming up.'

Soula's voice got louder. 'If your little brother

wasn't a pain, he wouldn't need that private school, would he?'

'So?' My tone matched hers. 'What do you expect me to do? Murder him or something?'

'What do you reckon!' Her fingers went tap, tap, tap against the phone. 'Ask your dad. I'll bet he gives it to you.'

'Good idea. I'll work on him tonight.' But this was mostly just to keep the peace.

That night I tried waiting up until Dad got home. But by the time he turned up, I was fast asleep. When Dad's here — and since he started the Pizzeria that isn't too often, he spends most of his waking hours in the garage where he's set up a kind of combined office and storeroom. First thing next morning, I found him at his desk sifting through a pile of paper. I quickly explained what I wanted.

'Sorry, love.' His face, round and plump like mine, looked so upset, my heart nearly missed a beat. 'Three hundred dollars isn't much. Only this month there's no cash to spare.' He pointed to a mountain of bills, then shrugged.

I frowned. 'But Dad, I thought we were doing

fine. I thought the pizzas were ... '

'Selling like hot cakes?' he finished off. 'They are. Only I borrowed plenty to set up the business. This week the bank tells me they want their money back, pronto. Next month, maybe I can give you something.' He peered at me and blinked. 'Why do you want to go to this camp? You're a fine figure of a girl. Not like the skinny little chickens who come into the pizza shop and act like they own the place ... '

'Don't worry, Dad,' I butted in before he could get onto one of his favourite topics. (Which is how rude some of the people who come into the Pizzeria are.) 'Soula and me. We'll find the money somehow.' I felt terrible for even asking.

But the very next day, as soon as I walked in the kitchen, Nonna handed me a big envelope. I stared at it in surprise.

'What's this, Nonna?' I asked her in Italian.

She shrugged, and continued chopping onions. I tore open the envelope. A heap of notes fell out. Scooping them up, I gaped in disbelief. Three hundred and fifty dollars in five and ten dollar notes. Nonna's savings. This must be part of Nonna's hard won savings ...

'Nonna, you're wonderful,' I screamed, throwing my arms around her and waltzing her around the kitchen, 'I'll pay you back as soon as possible. I promise, I promise ...'

Right then, the phone rang. I rushed to answer it.

'Dad's lending me three hundred dollars,' Soula shrieked in my ear.

'Nonna too,' I yelled back.

There was a bewildered pause before Soula asked, 'Nonna too, what?'

'Nonna's loaning me the money...'

'... isn't she terrific!' we screamed in unison.

We posted the cheque to Camp Avalon first thing next day.

Chapter 8

C amp Avalon turned out to be a sprawling old house in one of the most beautiful settings I've ever seen. Built in the foothills of the Great Dividing Range, the camp overlooked a beautiful dam and backed onto hectares and hectares of wonderful untouched bushland.

As Mrs Angelopolous drove up the circular drive a slim figure trotted out to meet us. I couldn't help staring. Whoever this guy was, he looked identical to the one on the Camp Avalon brochure ...

'Welcome to Camp Avalon,' he called, holding out his hand and smiling. 'I'm Ben, Ben Heineman. Your companionable, comradely, convivial guide.'

As we stared even more, he grinned and added, 'Companionable, comradely and convivial. It's our unofficial camp motto.'

Soula's eyes met mine. From their panicky expression I could tell she was wondering if living with such a gorgeous hunk would make us feel worse than ever? Even fatter and more unattractive than we were feeling right now?

Fighting down the terror, we helped Mrs Angelopolous take our bags out of the boot. Then Soula and I kissed her goodbye, and watched the car roll back down the drive and onto the highway. For a terrible moment I wondered if we weren't making a terrible mistake letting her leave without us ...

But before we had a chance to get too petrified, Ben took us inside. We dropped our bags in the front hall and went into the office to register our names. The office was empty, it turned out we were among the first to arrive, so Ben signed us in, then took us on a guided tour.

The first thing that struck me was how everything seemed brand new. It turned out that the building had been recently renovated.

'This,' Ben explained, 'is where all the main activities take place.' He showed us the lecture rooms, the dining-room, the Phys. Ed. rooms then took us into a sprawling living-room which had two table tennis tables, a large billiard table and loads of low comfy couches and coffee tables.

As we looked around, Soula asked Ben if he knew anything about the building's history.

'A bit.' He pushed open the doors to let us through. 'This used to be a posh hotel. In those days the licencing laws were so weird, if people wanted a glass of wine with their Sunday lunch, they had to drive thirty kilometres out of Melbourne to get it.'

Soula's eyes nearly popped out of her head. 'You mean, the law actually forced people to drink and drive?'

Ben laughed at her shocked expression. 'Maybe it wasn't as bad as it sounds. I mean, in those days there weren't nearly as many cars on the road, were there?'

The modern wing where everyone slept was tacked onto the back of the main building. As he led us to our room, he filled us in on some of the Camp's routine. 'We get you up early. Real early.'

'How early?' I asked suspiciously.

'Oh, round about dawn.' He grinned at our expressions.

'What happens then?'

'We go for a run.'

I managed to keep my groan down to a dull roar. 'And after that?'

'Then you get to do some serious exercise.'

Though I pretended to realise he was joking, secretly I was ready to pick up my bags and rush straight home.

'What about the people who run the place? What are they like?' Soula asked.

'They're great. Agnes Drabble's our boss. She's a medical doctor who specialises in kids with eating disorders. There's our two nurses Meg and Rob. Jim, who's in charge of Recreation and Physical Activities, and Cindy our dietician. Plus there's Con and me. We're supposed to act as buffers between you and the staff. Make you feel at home.'

Though I nodded, it sounded like a lot of people just to help us lose weight.

Just checking, I asked, 'How many kids are you expecting?'

'Fifty-three. It's heaps, but we're hoping you'll all be mates.'

Though Soula and I smiled politely, deep down somewhere I was really scared. So many people for us to know! How would I ever manage to remember fifty-three faces, fifty-three names, in just two weeks? From Soula's anxious expression, I could tell she was thinking the same ...

Maybe we would've got ourselves into a real state, even seriously considered ringing Mrs Angelopolous to come back and take us home, only Ben changed the subject to something more familiar.

'Hey, you two still at school?'

'Uh-huh.' Soula answered for us both. 'Starting Year 12 this year.'

'Lucky you!'

From Ben's laugh we knew he was safely beyond it. What interested me was that he didn't look too much older than us. Determined to find out more about him, I said, 'You were lucky to get this job.'

He smiled like he knew what I was thinking. 'Wasn't I? I did Year 12 the year before last. I've just completed my first year of a Recreation degree. This is my third visit to Camp Avalon, but my first job here. This way I get to earn money, help other people with similar problems, and have a great holiday myself.'

He was completely honest about once having been really overweight himself.

'I was so fat you wouldn't believe,' he grinned. 'Remind me to show a "before and after" photo, will you? It's taken me heaps of time to get into shape. Now I spend a couple of hours each day working out so I stay that way.'

Hearing how Ben once had problems like ours, helped Soula relax. She started firing questions: How did Ben get so thin? What did he eat? What did he do to stay in shape?

In no time flat the two of them were chatting

away like old mates. They didn't even notice I was still around.

Figuring I had two long weeks to learn about diet, exercise and weight loss, I tuned out of their conversation. These weird thoughts kept churning round and round in my mind. Soula and me had worked so hard at getting here, it'd all been such a tremendous effort. But now it seemed like none of this was happening, that all of this was just a dream, that we'd wandered onto the set of a Hollywood movie, everything was just too perfect.

Take Ben for example. Up this close, with those big green eyes, short blond hair and athletic looking body, he was even better-looking than I'd first realised. It was hard to remember he'd once been an ordinary overweight kid like Soula and me. What's more, he seemed like a sensitive, considerate person. Someone you'd really enjoy knowing.

Then, when I *did* finally join into their conversation, watching Soula act like Ben was the best thing she'd come across since sliced bread, I had to stop myself from shouting at her, or getting up and running out of the room ...

What if she got keen on Ben and forgot about Gerard Moloney? What if she forgot why we were here? Suddenly I realised it was too late. Soula was so caught up with Ben, in what he was saying, she wouldn't have noticed if I'd walked away, disappeared off the planet entirely. For a terrible moment I didn't know what to think.

Maybe I *was* a bit jealous. Soula and me had always been so close. I couldn't help wondering: If she got a proper boyfriend, would he come between us? Watching her and Ben made me feel stranger than ever. Not that I personally was attracted to Ben, or even hated the idea of him liking Soula. What was bothering me was far more complicated.

You see, if it took so little for Soula to forget Gerard, what would it take for me to forget Guy? And if I forgot Guy, who else would I have to daydream about, to always have in my mind, to work so hard for?

Maybe I should explain that I've been rapt in Guy forever, ever since we were both in third grade. I can still remember the day I first realised it. Our teacher was called Miss Raphael. Because she was young and inexperienced, we spent most of our lessons colouring in pictures. Basically this meant that a box filled with pencils was our most important piece of school equipment. The problem was that our class had heaps of bullies, and because I was a fat little kid who found it hard to fight back, those bullies picked on me every chance they got.

One day, Miss Raphael left the room for five minutes, so as usual I was in tears. Gerard (yes the same Gerard that Soula likes so much) had stolen my pencil case and was throwing my pencils all around the room. Suddenly Guy saw me. He must've felt sorry for me or something, because he suddenly stood up to Gerard, told him that if he didn't stop teasing Mia Spanetti, he'd bash him up.

Gerard stared back. 'Yeah? So I'll bash you back!'

What followed was the biggest fight ever. Gerard gave Guy a blood nose, so I guess he won in the end. But as far as I was concerned, it wouldn't have mattered who won that fight. I was in love with Guy the moment he stood up for me, and I've never recovered.

So you can also see why, without Guy to think about, I'm left with a case of permanent fright. Which in turn leaves that hollow inside. And as it's the kind of hollow which makes me long for potato cakes, Tim Tams, cream cakes and big slabs of milk chocolate, I was even more determined to hang onto thoughts of Guy.

While all this went puffing through my mind like an old steam train, while Ben and Soula were chatting away like mad, we eventually got to our room. Forty-three, said the number on the door. I pushed it open. Inside there was just enough space for two built-in wardrobes, a couple of beds, a tiny desk, a chair and two doors ... one leading to the corridor and the other to a tiny bathroom we shared with the adjoining room.

'Rebecca and Kirsty are your neighbours,' Ben said. 'It's none of my business, but with you four guys sharing the bathroom, you might try working out a roster.'

Just as I was think that this sounded like good advice, a guy with dark hair poked his head around the door.

'Con!' Ben waved him inside. 'Come and meet Soula and Mia.'

'Hi Soula, Mia!'

Con flopped onto the bed and stared hard at us. As his stare was more like he wanted to remember exactly what we looked like than someone being rude, I just stared back.

Something about Con seemed familar. Almost as if I'd met him somewhere before only I couldn't think where. Because I was used to comparing every guy I met with Guy, I started doing that with Con. He wasn't nearly as handsome. Con's features were definitely coarser than Guy's. And where Guy was fair and had blue, blue eyes, Con's eyes were black, his complexion dark enough for him to have a permanent five o'clock shadow, and he was quite a bit shorter.

I guess Con would've been considered better looking if his nose hadn't met with a terrible accident — it was flattened in the centre. But it was obvious how hard he worked at developing his muscles; you could tell from the way they bulged through his Camp Avalon tracksuit that he did heaps of work-outs. So though he didn't have the same groovy appearance as Guy or Ben, I figured most girls would describe him as a spunk.

When he noticed me checking him out, Con leaned forward and smiled. I felt myself blush. Once I recovered from my embarrassment, I had to admit that Con's smile was nice. Shy but nice. The smile of someone who would never push himself too far forward or be obnoxious. He waved at Ben. 'Don't let him feed you too much garbage, will you.'

Ben laughed. 'Con and I met the year before last. You wouldn't believe what a real slob he was.'

Con made a face, then laughed. 'Only because I grew up in a family which thinks you should eat all you can in case there's a famine coming.'

I got so excited, I almost forgot to be shy. 'My dad thinks that way!' I said. 'And it's exactly like my Nonna.'

'By Nonna, Mia means her grandmother,' Soula explained.

I nodded. 'Nonna used to get so mad if I didn't finish everything on my plate, I just didn't dare.'

Con and I grinned at each other.

I guess we could've kept on grinning, except Ben interrupted with, 'That's why we're here. To change those terrible eating habits we learnt as little kids.'

Con laughed. His laugh was really great, I decided. Warm and friendly. Like he really liked people. I slowly smiled back. We smiled at each other. Con suddenly asked, 'Are you a happy or sad kind of person?'

I frowned. 'What do you mean, happy or sad?'

'Like I said. What are you? Are you mostly happy or sad?'

'Happy, I guess. Right now I'm happy to be here.'

'Great,' he laughed, and we all joined in.

It was such a relief, I can't tell you. It was so good knowing those guys understood exactly how we felt. They didn't hold it against Soula and me that we didn't have perfect proportions, or didn't look like Madonna or Cher. They'd been through it all themselves, and they knew what it was like to feel different in the wrong kind of way, to know you didn't make the grade, to always feel like an outsider, to wish people would stop staring at your shape instead of looking at who you *really* are.

What the hell, I thought. This has got to be better than anything that's happened to us before. After all, when you've been down in the dumps for as long as we have, the only way out is up.

Chapter 9

After explaining that it was time for them to get back to work, Ben and Con left, and Soula and I started settling in.

I was lying flat on my back, just checking out the beds, when someone tapped on the door which led to the corridor. Soula was still unpacking, so I hopped up to answer it.

A girl, around my age, was standing on the other side of the door.

'I'm Rebecca.' She held out her hand. 'You two share the bathroom with Kirsty and me.'

'Hi!' Hoping my smile hid my disbelieving

stare, I reached out and shook her hand. 'I'm Mia. this is Soula.'

Rebecca was so skinny, I could hardly believe it. Her head was like a skull, her ribs were outlined by her jumper, her arms and legs were like matchsticks and her skin was so pale it was almost see-through. What on earth was someone who looked like they'd just come from Ethiopia doing at a camp for fat kids?

Suddenly the bathroom door burst open. Rebecca's roommate, Kirsty, swayed into the room on short little dumpling feet.

My jaw dropped even further. Fortunately Soula, even if she was secretly amazed at seeing someone as huge as Kirsty, didn't twitch a muscle. She invited Kirsty to sit on her bed. Then, ignoring the way the bed sagged under so much weight, and how long it took Kirsty to get herself settled, she talked to the other two about Camp Avalon, about how nice she thought Ben and Con were, about how much we'd been looking forward to coming here.

Once she got herself comfortable, Kirsty started firing questions at Soula and me.

'What schools are you at?'

'Donyvale.' I answered for us both. 'We're starting Year 12 when we go back.'

Kirsty laughed. 'Yeah?' Her double chins wobbled. Later, when I got to know her better, I'd always remember Kirsty for her low laughter. 'So are we. In Year 12, I mean. What subjects are you doing?'

'English, maths, biology, chemistry, and home economics ... '

' ... except I'm taking physics instead of home economics,' Soula butted in.

Kirsty turned to look at Soula. 'Maths and science, eh? You two must be pretty smart.'

Soula groaned and said, 'Sometimes I wonder. Maths and science! They're a hell of a lot of work.'

'I was doing those subjects,' Rebecca said to me in her little-girl voice, 'only I ended up missing too much school to keep up my maths.'

I nodded like I understood, but I was really curious. Why had she missed so much school? Why was she so thin? Then it suddenly struck me that maybe Rebecca was recovering from a terrible illness. But what sort of disease made you look like a refugee from a famine?

Though these thoughts were running through my mind, I must have said the right sorts of things, because Rebecca immediately offered to take us down the passage to a tiny pantry where we could help ourselves to tea and coffee.

When we got there, I checked out the contents of the shelves, then groaned to myself. The coffee was made from barley and chicory, all the teas were herbal, there was no sugar, the milk was low-fat, and though I searched high and low there wasn't a biscuit to be seen.

'Okay, okay, so we'll all starve to death,' said Soula. 'At least the water's hot.'

After the four of us settled back in our room, we spent ages talking about school and the universities we hoped to get into next year. After a while Soula and I opened up about our families, our hobbies, our likes and dislikes. We both laid off talking about Guy and Gerard though. I guess if they'd been anyone else we might've mentioned those guys. I mean, normally Guy and Gerard take up heaps of our conversation — only Kirsty made it clear from the start that she wasn't interested in men.

'There's no point in someone like me liking a guy,' she said. 'Men are only interested in what a girl looks like.'

And Rebecca, in that funny voice which made her sound like she was ten instead of seventeen, backed this up by saying, 'Men want women who look like cover girls. You look too diferent, and they don't want to know you.'

Soula and I nodded politely. Not that I actually agreed with this sentiment, but who was I to argue? The facts were that we were here to lose weight, so when we got back home Guy and Gerard would (hopefully) find both of us irresistible. At the same time I had this terrible urge to argue with Kirsty, to point out there was more to being friendly with men than just looks. I mean, men are human too, aren't they? So doesn't it follow that they'd want some of the same things we want? Like friendship? Warmth?

But if I'd ever thought Soula and I had weight problems, I didn't know the half. It turned out that both Rebecca and Kirsty were suffering from horrendous eating disorders. The kind of illness that killed people.

'I've got Anorexia Nervosa,' Rebecca confided. 'And Kirsty's Bulemic. We met up in hospital. We're calling this "our last chance corral". If we don't start losing weight pretty soon, the doctors keep threatening to send us back in.'

Soula couldn't help saying, 'Rebecca! Don't tell me they expect you to lose more weight? There'll be nothing left of you! Shouldn't you be trying to put it on?'

'Hmm.' Rebecca wouldn't meet her eye. 'I guess so. Only it's really so hard ... '

'Hard? I butted in. 'Being forced to eat cakes and chocolate and stuff? You've got to be kidding.'

'Not you, too.' Rebecca jumped up and started for her room. 'That's what everyone says. You all want me to look grosser than I do right now... '

'Hey, that's not what I meant at all ... '

Too late. She slammed the door behind her.

I felt terrible. What had I done? No one said anything.

I turned to Kirsty, 'I'm so sorry. I didn't mean

to upset Rebecca.'

Kirsty shrugged her massive shoulders. 'You see,' she explained as the bed lurched dangerously underneath her, 'with Anorexia, it doesn't matter how thin you are, you always see yourself as fat. When it comes to talking about weight, you have to be dead careful of what you say in front of Rebecca.'

Later, heading for the dining room, Soula whispered in my ear, 'Maybe this isn't going to be as simple as we thought.'

I rolled my eyes. 'What made you think it would be?'

She didn't bother answering.

Chapter 10

S eated in the dining room at one of the long tables, we had a chance to look over the staff and most of the other people. The staff was young, younger than most of our teachers at Donyvale, and most of the kids were younger than Soula and me. And I counted twice as many girls as guys. Did that mean girls got fatter than guys? But maybe having so many more girls here than guys meant that we were just more self-conscious about our looks ...

I looked around carefully. Though most of the people were really overweight, no one else was as big as Kirsty. Nor was Rebecca the only girl suffering from Anorexia Nervosa.

Though I'd been preparing myself for a meal of lettuce leaves and raw carrots, I was really curious about what we would have dished up for dinner. In the last few months, Soula and I had made heaps of jokes about living on dry crusts and a small bowl of spinach. But what they served was really delicious. Our meal included stir fry beef, one small potato baked in its jacket, beans, broccoli and carrots, plus heaps of salad. And for dessert? Peaches set in diet-jelly.

All the same you couldn't help noticing how carefully each portion was doled out. And to be perfectly honest, with lunch in Melbourne being more than five hours away, even after we finished eating, I could've still eaten a horse.

'What I'd give for a couple of packets of potato chips and Tim Tams,' I whispered in Soula's ear.

'Just shut your mouth,' she grinned. And ran her finger over her throat in a cutting motion.

All through dinner, I kept one eye on the food and another on Ben and Con. While everyone else ate dinner, they kept hopping up from their seats, wandering between tables, talking to everyone in the room, introducing shy looking people to each other, trying hard to make everyone feel at home. Though I suspected it was easier for Ben than for Con to act friendly, they were both making a great effort to make the situation less stressful for everyone.

I couldn't help comparing *their* manners with Guy and Gerard's. Because although Ben and Con laughed and joked all the time, and everyone could see how friendly they were and how much they liked being here, I could just imagine how awkward and shy our guys would've been in this environment. I mean, neither Guy, and certainly not Gerard, would have much patience for people they'd think of as freaky.

Half way through the meal, a very slim, athletic looking, dark haired lady around Mum's age stood up and introduced herself as Dr Agnes Drabble, the camp director.

'I want to welcome all of you to Camp Avalon,' she said, and went on to introduce her staff. She finished up very carefully spelling out the rules.

'We try to limit them, but we keep those very strictly. The most important one is that there's no moving off the camp grounds without permission from me. If anyone is caught leaving the grounds,' she glanced warningly around, 'they'll automatically be expelled.'

'So above all don't get caught!' Con's voice came from the back of the room.

Everyone laughed. So did Dr Drabble. But something in her expression told me she meant every word she'd said.

Chapter 11

That first week rushed by, literally! Most of the time I was absolutely exhausted, my muscles sore from so much exercise and, until I got used to their newer, different style of eating, absolutely ravenous for my favourite foods.

At night, instead of my usual dreams of Guy, I was haunted by visions of hamburgers, pizzas, hot chips, potato cakes, bread sticks covered in runny butter and honey, jam doughnuts, cheese cake, Cherry Ripes, Tim Tams, and chocolate Teddy Bears.

First thing each morning when a loud bell woke us, we'd pull on our T-shirts and shorts, jog down the drive to the road and along a quiet bush track. Running or Power Walking for three-quarters of an hour, we often covered anything up to eight kilometres before going back to our rooms to shower and change.

Then breakfast. It was always the same: one piece of fresh fruit, a small bowl of untoasted muesli covered in low-fat milk, and one slice of wholemeal toast with a tiny scraping of butter and vegemite.

Our third morning there, Soula grumbled, 'I'll be sick if I have to eat. I can't face food first off.'

Ben, sitting next to her, nodded sympathetically. 'Neither could I. My starter used to be a mug of strong coffee and mayble a couple of sweet biscuits. By mid-morning I'd be hungry enough to eat a horse, so I'd fill up on junk.'

'Uh-huh, me too,' Soula sighed. From her expression, you might've thought she and Ben were discussing love poetry instead of debating which cereals were best. 'Hot chips and Mars Bars is what we usually got ...'

'Hot chips and Mars Bars,' I groaned. 'What I'd give for a bag of hot greasy chips right now...'

I could've been talking from the moon the amount of attention this got.

'The secret is complex carbohydrates,' Ben was telling Soula — by now they were so close, she was practically sitting on his knee. 'That way your body burns up calories very slowly, and you don't get so peckish.'

And then he kissed her! I couldn't believe it! And they spent the rest of the meal smiling at each other in between gulping down muesli and freshly squeezed orange juice.

Now I don't want to give you the impression I was jealous. I mean, I was really pleased for Soula, pleased she'd gotten over Gerard (who always treated her so badly), pleased she now had Ben. But the thing was ... whenever I was with them, I felt about as welcome as a blowfly at a barbecue.

I spent the rest of the day wondering who's idea it'd been to come to Camp Avalon in the first place. In the end I got so depressed, I had to remind myself *why* I was here, remind myself how amazed Guy would be when he first caught sight of the new gorgeous Mia Spanetti.

Breakfast over, the rest of the morning was spent being individually checked out, weighed and assessed by the staff. Because of my interest in the hospitality business, I got to know Cindy, the Camp dietician.

Cindy was a very attractive, long-legged blonde in her late twenties.

Our first week there, she said to me, 'You've actually got a very fine bone structure. Lose twelve kilos and you'll be healthier, you'll look great and I promise you'll have heaps more energy.'

'Saying's one thing, doing's another,' I said. 'I'm starving hungry all the time.'

If I was looking for sympathy, Cindy was the last person to give it. 'If you're eating everything we serve,' she said, 'you're getting enough kilojoules. And,' she added, 'if you still feel hungry, it's only because your stomach's too used to being stuffed. The best thing for you is to nibble on carrot and celery chips. They're high in fibre and low in kilojoules so you won't put on weight.'

'Wouldn't you know it. Carrot and celery chips. What I'd give for some hot potato chips right now ... '

One look from her, and I quickly shut up. Anyway, something more important was on my mind. 'This new kind of eating. It kind of messes me up. Career wise, I mean.'

Though Cindy was busy checking the next day's menu, she glanced up in surprise. 'Why?'

I explained, 'I was going into the hospitality business. All this,' I waved my arms at her diet, the kitchen, the whole new way of eating, 'doesn't fit in.'

Cindy's eyebrows shot up. 'You're absolutely wrong,' she said. 'Eating this way is how the hospitality business is going. You're much more likely to get a job if you learn to cook like us.'

When we weren't having our fat cells discussed, or being tested for diabetes or high cholesterol counts or some obscure thyroid deficiencies, we were sent into small tutorial groups. The staff took turns in lecturing us on what damage we were doing to our bodies by not eating sensibly or getting enough exercise. Not that the message was always negative. For example, they spent a lot of time helping us work out strategies for coping with our daily lives, planning sensible eating and exercise routines. But the best was when Cindy took me into the kitchens and showed me how to cook tasty, satisfying food that was low in sugars and fats.

As the weeks went on, we soon learnt that successful weight loss didn't mean total starvation.

'Keeping to the right weight for your height and body type shouldn't mean deprivation and hunger,' Dr Drabble explained. 'Mostly it's a case of changing bad eating habits to more sensible ones. Then, if you do occasionally pig out, it won't matter too much. But if you starve your body with crazy diets, it thinks famine times have come and it starts using energy very sparingly. Basically, that's why so much dieting doesn't work. Because when you *do* start eating differently, your body hangs onto all that extra fat in case there's another famine.

'Depending on your activity level, the body only uses a certain amount of energy. Let's put it this way; a long distance runner will use five times as much energy as a student sitting at his desk. I'll give you another example ... every hundred grams of chocolate needs two hours of brisk walking to burn it off. And because chocolate is mostly refined carbohydrates and fat, you end up hungry. Too much chocolate and, sooner or later, those excess kilos start to show.' She stared round the room. 'You all following this?'

We nodded to show we were.

When Dr Drabble's lecture finally ended, I headed for the dining room. I'd finished helping myself to lunch, and was waiting for Soula to collect hers, when Con walked over. 'Hi, Mia. Come and eat with me.'

I admit I was surprised at him singling me out. Though we'd spent heaps of time together, until now it was always with other people. Things were like that here. Unless, like Ben and Soula, you were part of an established twosome, most of the kids, even the really shy ones, stayed within a group.

Wondering what Con had to say that was so strictly confidential, I followed him to a table set slightly apart from the others. We sat opposite each other and started eating. As I dug into my salad I was conscious of how often in the last few days I'd looked up to find his eyes on me. Not that his gaze was unpleasant or anything like that, but I kept wondering why he was so interested in watching what I got up to?

Then, inevitably, I started comparing Con with Guy, contrasting my feelings for the two.

Though I liked Con heaps, I wasn't in love with him, not like I was with Guy. But apart from Con's enormous energy he had other qualities I admired. For example, when someone was holding the floor, he mostly stayed silent. But he was a terrific listener. And the way he concentrated on what the talker had to say, I knew he enjoyed hearing differing points of view.

This was something I really appreciated. It meant I never had to work hard at holding his attention. I mean, not like I did with Guy. What's more, Con didn't seem to mind those times I didn't feel like talking. He could sit for hours in silence, and you never felt uncomfortable. And the way his eyes kept meeting mine, like he was hoping to meet with my approval instead of the other way round, was really flattering.

We spent the first part of the meal just munching away on our food. When Con did open up, the subject was unexpected.

'You watch much TV?'

I smiled. 'What do you mean by much?'

'Well, do you watch soapies?'

'Some,' I admitted. 'I watch "Chances" and "Home and Away". They help me relax. When I watch soapies I kind of switch off thinking.'

He smiled. I liked the way the corners of his eyes crinkled when he smiled. 'Me too. Only at our place it gets pretty hard. Whenever I get interested, Evie, my little sister, and Mum come into the room and interrupt.'

My ears pricked up. 'Doesn't your mum like tellie?'

He blushed a bit. 'It's just that she doesn't speak much English, so she's always at me to tell her what's going on.'

I grinned. 'Same here. My Nonna speaks so little English it's a wonder she manages to do anything, like shopping and stuff.'

'Yeah.' He knew what I meant. 'Not having the language must be hard.'

'I reckon. Whenever I try and get Nonna to learn some English, she says old dogs don't learn new tricks.'

'They must've got together, because that's what my mum says.'

'When did your folks get here?'

'When I was little.' He forked in a mouthful of lettuce and chewed on it. 'What about yours?'

'I was born here — but only just. Poor Nonna. It must be hard not really understanding anything that's going on.'

He nodded. There was a longish pause. Though I usually didn't mind us not talking, this time the silence was awkward; like there was something he wanted to say, only suddenly wasn't sure how. I stared round the room. Though almost everyone else had finished lunch, were standing up, beginning to leave, Con looked really settled in.

I finished my lunch.

Eventually I got around to asking, 'Do you like reading?'

He considered this like it was really important. 'A bit,' he said in the end. 'I like reading science fiction and fantasy. Mostly I don't get too much time. How about you?'

'Me? I read heaps. I really like books, I read stacks of novels. But if I haven't got one handy, I'll read anything else ... you know, the back of the cereal packet, ads, other people's newspapers on the tram, and if I'm really desperate, even stuff from school.'

He laughed, then said, 'What about films? You like watching videos?'

'Horror,' I said, 'I really dig funny horror movies.'

'Like *I was a Teenage Werewolf*?'

'Yeah! What about *Young Frankenstein*?'

'Or *Childsplay*? Did you ever get to see that?'

'Did I ever. Parts one *and* two. Only I reckon they're too sick to be funny.'

'What about *Silence of the Lambs*?'

'Yuk!' I shuddered. 'Murder and cannibilism? That's too horrible to watch.'

'I agree. There's so much real life horror out there, who wants it as entertainment.'

Right then Soula and Ben floated past. They waved. I waved back. When I turned back to Con, his eyes were glued on me. I blushed. Con was acting like he was really interested. Keen on Mia Spanetti? Poor Con! All I could think was if he liked *me*, there had to be something really wrong with *him*.

With this in mind, I got up, smiled, and took my dirty plates and cutlery back to the counter.

Chapter 12

'**Y**ou've lost over four kilos!'

I stared at the scales in disbelief. According to them, I'd lost over half a stone in less than a week. And in case I suspected they were wrong, there was heaps of other evidence to prove it was true; my clothes felt looser, my body less lumpy, my silhouette was definitely trimmer. Whenever I went to fix my hair, I barely recognised myself. The mirror showed larger eyes, less puffy cheeks, even skinnier nose and ears.

With only eight kilos to lose to reach my final

goal, I started to get excited.

'At this rate,' I said to Kirsty, who was next in line to be weighed, 'You'll see my cheekbones at last. We'll be slim, svelte and soignee by the time we're back at school.'

Kirsty laughed. 'What does soignee mean?'

'It's French for really cool.'

Kirsty just stared at herself. Today, in preparation for yet another aerobics session, both of us were in leotards and joggers. I grinned at her reflection. Being perfectly honest, neither of us looked too soignee as yet.

Give it time, I reminded myself. Give it time …

'Aerobics, jogging and lectures in the morning,' Kirsty sighed.

' …and squash, tennis, swimming, rowing and netball in the afternoon.'

'And not a minute to ourselves. It's all so exhausting, I'm absolutely beat. Stuffed. Burnt-out. Dead.' Proving she meant it, Kirsty's yawn was so broad, I could almost see her tonsils.

'Me too,' I admitted. 'But it's certainly worth it. Look at what great shapes we're becoming.'

Kirsty shook her head. 'Maybe *you'll* end up

a great shape. Not me. I like food too much. I'll never make it.'

I stared at her. 'Of course you will,' I protested, but she kept on shaking her head in this really negative way.

As there didn't seem much point arguing, I tucked my hand into her arm, and we set off for the gymnasium. Not that Soula had given me up for dead or anything like that, but right now I was grateful to have Kirsty and Rebecca as my friends.

'It's just that she's so rapt in Ben, there's no room left for anyone else,' I explained as Kirsty and I walked slowly down the corridor. 'It feels so weird. Until now, we've always done everything together. We went to school together, cooked together, chased guys together. But now, I'm not really sure of what I want ...'

Realising how selfish this sounded, my voice trailed off. But Kirsty understood.

'I know, I know!' Her double chins wobbled. 'You're really pleased your friend's got a guy, but you miss her all the same. That's how it was with me when Rebecca was going out with Sam.'

My eyes widened. 'I didn't know Rebecca's got a boyfriend?'

'She hasn't. At least, not any more. It's a really sad story.' Kirsty took a couple more steps, then paused to catch her breath. 'Rebecca was keen on Sam. Much keener than he was on her. After he dropped her for Maria, she stopped eating. Because Maria used to do some part-time modelling, I guess Rebecca thought that if *she* looked more like a model, Sam would come back to her. Of course he didn't but by then it was too late. She'd already developed anorexia.'

'Poor Rebecca! Does she know how dangerous her disease is? I mean, it could kill her, couldn't it?'

'I'm sure she does. It's just that the urge not to eat is even stronger.' Rounding the corner, we headed up the passage. 'How are you getting on with Con?'

I blushed a bit. 'What do you mean, how am I getting on with Con?'

'Every time I look for you, I see *him* hanging around.'

'Doesn't mean anything,' I said. 'He's just

being friendly. He works hard at being nice.'

'You still finding him hard to talk to?'

'No.' I shook my head. 'Not any more. I'm getting used to the strong silent type. Actually,' I admitted, 'it's really kind of peaceful. I never have to make an effort to keep him entertained.'

Kirsty laughed, but all she said was, 'Con's really nice. And attractive *and* intelligent. What's more, I think he really likes you. Remember that old saying? Don't cut off your nose to spite your face?'

'I don't know what you're talking about,' I said, laughing her off. But seeing I'd spent several hours just the day before boring her and Rebecca with endless stories about Guy Prescott, of course I did.

My problem was that though I thought of Con as a nice, intelligent, attractive guy, any time I thought seriously about tossing over Guy for him, I immediately got this empty feeling inside. I told myself I wasn't as attracted to Con as I was to Guy. I wasn't in love with Con.

Maybe it was just that, even though I liked Con a lot, I felt none of the agony I'd built up over the years for Guy. And, like a habit that's hard to break, I was used to longing. While Guy was, at least so far, unattainable, he was the most wonderful challenge in the world. Con, on the other hand, was only waiting for me to give the okay.

So what was wrong with Con?

Anyway, what would I do with a real live boyfriend? All in all it seemed easier to remind myself I didn't really like Con enough to change my thinking around.

Chapter 13

On our second Saturday night, the night before we were due to go home, Camp Avalon held a big dance. I guess I should've been looking forward to the night more than I was. For once I didn't have to worry about my clothes being tight, or looking terrible, or Guy not taking any notice of me.

But as Soula would be totally preoccupied with Ben, in a way it was like being at my first dance ever. I kept wondering what it would be like. You see, by this second week, though I knew most of the kids by name, even knew some of them, like

Kirsty and Rebecca, pretty intimately, I was still scared of turning up by myself.

What if I was left standing by the wall, no one wanting to talk to me? What if no one wanted to dance with me?

I mean, these things had happened to me often enough in the past. The only difference was that in those days I had Soula and she had me. We propped each other up, pretended we didn't care that none of the guys liked us enough to ask us to dance. 'Only a matter of time,' we kept telling each other, 'and they'll realise how great we really are.'

When I got to the games room where the dance was being held, Kirsty and Rebecca weren't there. It was then I realised I hadn't seen either of them since lunch.

My heart sank. Where were they? Maybe they weren't coming? I started to feel anxious. By now, by the end of this second week of camp, it was unusual for us not to be in constant contact …

Then I forgot about them almost straight away, because the music kicked off. To my surprise I started having a really great time. When Con caught my eye, we danced opposite each other. Con was a terrific dancer. Most people are surprised at how well some fat people move. But let a fatty lose weight, and it's really amazing how much better he or she becomes, how much longer they can keep going, how well they tune into the beat. Since I'd lost six kilos, half my goal weight, I had lots more energy and I was feeling heaps more attractive. Moving was so much easier, I could scarcely believe it.

Half way through the next song Con shouted in my ear.

'Time for a break?'

'Right!' I grinned. 'Time for a Kit Kat?'

'Nope.' He shook his head. 'Kit Kats are out. At least, for us.'

We wandered outside and stared up at the stars. I had never seen them so close. The air felt fresh and tingly. I took a deep breath, filling my lungs with the scent of eucalypts and damp earth. Being in the country was great. One day, I told myself, I'd like to work in the country, maybe move here on a permanent basis ...

Con broke into my thoughts, 'Want to walk?'

I nodded. We set off down the drive. There was another of those long silences between us. Only this time I didn't let it worry me. Con, I already knew, didn't need entertaining.

A shame it was so much harder being with Guy!

The thought flitted disobediently through my mind.

Chasing it away, I reminded myself that this was something that helped make Guy so attractive. Guy was my challenge, my goal, my dream ...

'Hard to believe all this'll be over by tomorrow,' Con suddenly said.

I stared up at him. Here, away from the building, it was so dark, I could barely make out his shape. 'What have you got planned for the rest of the break?'

'A job at the local gym.'

'Sounds okay.'

'You reckon? Sweeping floors, scrubbing down walls and swimming pools?' But his tone was light, so I guessed he didn't mind too much.

'Yuk! Maybe not so okay.'

'Well ...' He paused. 'Jobs are scarce, so I

suppose it's better than nothing. What are you doing?'

'Mum needs a break so I'm going into the Pizzeria with Dad. He says if I'm really interested in catering as a career, I need heaps more experience.'

'Uh-huh.' We got to the end of the drive and turned back. By now, though I was used to Con's long silences, I could tell something was up. But we were almost at the house before he said, 'Mia, you reckon you could find time to see me? You see, I really like you heaps ...' his voice trailed off.

I just stared at him. It was so dark I could just make out his shape. What was I supposed to say. Let's face it, who but a real drip would be attracted to someone as unappealing as me? There must be another, more unscrupulous motive behind all this. I wished I knew what it was. Then it struck me that maybe he thought fat girls didn't have to be taken seriously as thin ones. Lots of guys think fat girls are easy. Maybe he thought he wouldn't have to watch himself like he would with someone thinner and more attractive?

And what about Guy? I hadn't forgotten why I'd come to Camp Avalon in the first place. If things were going to work out the way I had them planned, after one look at me, Guy would be eating out of my hand. Then who'd have time for Con?

'That'd be great,' I managed to stammer. 'Only I've got all this reading to do. You know, school stuff and all that. And Dad's expecting me to work long hours. One way and another the next few months'll be pretty busy ...'

'It's okay,' Con said quietly. 'Soula told me all about him.'

'Told you about who?' My voiced seemed to have gone a bit squeaky. What right did Soula have to discuss my affairs without asking my permission first?

'That you're keen on this Guy Prescott. That you've been in love with him for years.'

Even though my mind was firmly made up, tears started rolling down my cheeks. 'You see,' I tried to explain while scrabbling in my pocket for a tissue, 'I've been in love with Guy for ages.

It's not like it's new, or anthing like that ...'

'It's okay.' Con said, but I could tell he was really upset. 'You don't have to apologise for liking someone else ...'

'But I do, I do,' I said. 'If I don't explain, you'll take it personally and you won't understand ...'

He laughed, but not like he was enjoying himself. 'It's a bit hard *not* taking it personally. This kind of knockback is a pretty personal matter.'

What a fool I was. Even if Con had a more dishonest reason for asking me out, the last thing I wanted was to antagonise him. Even if he couldn't ever, ever replace Guy, by now I liked him too much to want to hurt his feelings. I really liked Con, I enjoyed his company, and I wanted us to stay friends. Back at the front door, tears were rolling down my cheeks. If only there was some way I could make us both feel better ...

But before I could think of anything sensible to say, there was a hurried, 'See you later,' and Con disappeared into the dark.

Chapter 14

After that, as there was no way I wanted to talk to anyone, I went straight to my room, stripped off my clothes, climbed into bed and turned my face to the wall.

After a while I was standing on a squashcourt watching Con and Guy play.

Because of the way they kept slamming the ball, you knew that they really wanted to hit each other instead of the ball. Only that wasn't the problem. The problem was me. Trapped in the middle of the court, dodging the ball, their racquets, them, I had to duck like mad or I would've been bruised all over. But no matter how hard I yelled for them to be more careful, they were taking absolutely no notice …

'Mia. Get up will you?'

Soula was shaking me awake.

'Huh?' I sat up with a jolt. 'What's wrong?'

'Kirsty and Rebecca are in trouble.'

'What happened?'

'You seen them today?'

'Sure. This morning. In the gym.' I rolled out of bed and stood shivering. 'Where are they now?'

'They were rostered to play netball this afternoon, but they didn't turn up. Seems they hitchhiked a lift into town. Cindy saw them in "The Pig and Whistle Tearooms". They asked her not to dob them in, but you know how tough she is. Soon as she got back she went straight to Dr Drabble.'

'Yeah?' I wrapped myself in my doona. 'What's the problem?'

Soula brushed her hair angrily. 'Honestly, Mia,' she said impatiently. 'You're being dim. You forgotten the rules? First, they're not allowed off the grounds without permission. Second, they were sitting in a cafe eating Devonshire tea.'

'Oh. What'll happen to them now?'

'Con says they'll be expelled.'

'So what's the big deal?' I yawned and looked longingly at my bed. 'We're all going home tomorrow, aren't we?'

'It's not as simple as all that. *We* might be going home tomorrow, but Kirsty and Rebecca will be sent back to hospital.'

I stared at Soula. 'Rebecca? Rebecca in trouble for eating afternoon tea? Everyone's desperate for her to eat.'

Soula laughed. 'Oh, Rebecca wasn't eating. She only went along to keep Kirsty company.'

'Hmm. So what happens now?'

'I dont know.' Soula's face crinkled. For a moment I thought she was about to cry. 'You know how you can hear everything going on in the main office? Con and Dr Drabble were in there, so I went and listened in. Con was pleading on their behalf. Dr Drabble got so wild. She told him that if he kept on protecting them he was undermining her authority, and he didn't have a hope of getting a job here next year.

What's more, she wouldn't even give him a decent reference so he could get one somewhere else.'

I was horrified. 'What did he do? Did he back down?'

Soula shrugged. 'Con's such a nice guy, I never realised he was so stubborn. He really lost his temper. He told Dr Drabble that he didn't agree with her one bit. He said she was far too strict, and that it was perfectly natural and normal for people to break those kinds of absolute rules. He said she should give the girls another chance and not tell the doctors.'

'Did Dr Drabble listen?'

'No. She just got madder than ever.'

I ducked through the bathroom and into Kirsty and Rebecca's room. Their beds were stripped, the wardrobe empty. From the room's bare look you'd never have known Kirsty and Rebecca had once lived in there.

What with one thing and another, I didn't sleep much more that night. I was worried about Kirsty and Rebecca, but what really kept going round and round in my mind was Con. If Con was only out to take advantage of fat girls like me, why would he put himself out for Kirsty and Rebecca? Surely only a really nice guy would stand up for his principles in the way Con had? Especially if it meant losing the job he had here.

Had I been too quick to tell Con I wasn't interested?

'Don't cut off your nose to spite your face.' Kirsty's words kept on echoing in my head.

I dozed off for a while, but I woke up well before the bell went for our early morning run. There was something important I had to do.

I pulled on my jogging gear. But instead of heading down the drive, I shot down the corridor to where Ben and Con shared a room.

I knocked hard on the door. It opened up a fraction. Ben peered out. 'Mia? What's up?'

'Where's Con? I really need to talk to him.'

Ben's sleepiness disappeared. He looked wide awake and angry. 'Con? Sacked. No chance of ever getting back. The idiot really got Dr Drabble going. They had a terrible blue over Kirsty and Rebecca. Con stormed out straight after.'

'He didn't leave any message for me?' I asked.

'Nope!' Ben shook his head. 'All he said was that the sooner he wiped Camp Avalon off his feet, the better he'd feel.'

'Oh,' I said. And as there didn't seem anything I could say without giving myself away, I left it at that.

Chapter 15

S oula's mum dropped me home. Voices were coming from the dining room, and I guessed the family was in there and half-way through lunch. After dropping my things in my room, I pushed open the door.

In the centre of the table, like an offering to a god of plenty, sat a gargatuan bowl of pasta smothered in Nonna's special tomato sauce and freshly grated parmesan cheese. Tony wasn't there (he was spending the weekend at a friend's) but Mum, Dad and Nonna were so involved with lunch, it took them a few seconds to realise I was home. Of course, as soon as they did, they jumped up, kissing and hugging me like I'd been away for at least a year.

Wasn't I lucky to have a such great family? Their welcoming faces were a sight for sore eyes. Then, just as I was thinking how good it was being home, a funny niggle ran down my spine.

Now this is almost too embarrassing to admit, but I'd forgotten how fat they were. Such apple round cheeks, roly poly bodies, fat sausage fingers ...

And it suddenly occurred to me that the three people I loved the most in the world could be heading for disaster ... a sudden coronary, gall stones, diabetes or even something worse? I stared at them in dismay.

Just as I was thinking this, Nonna picked up an extra large plate, filled it with a mountain of tagliatelli and plonked it in front of me.

'Not so much. Nonna, I don't eat so much any more,' I said.

Too late. Nonna was muttering, only half to herself, 'Look at her. Nothing there. She'll get sick. Just skin and bones. All dried up. Almost nothing left ...'

'Nonna's right!' Dad's eyebrows shot into his head. 'Mia looks like a plucked chook, like the girls who come into the Pizzeria.' A forkfull of tagliatelli halfway to his mouth, he ordered in Italian, 'Maria, get her eating right away.'

Though I was hungry enough to eat a hippopotamus, I shoved the contents of my plate back into the bowl. How could they talk like I wasn't there? Didn't Nonna and Dad realise how hard I'd worked to lose this weight? And now, instead of offering me their congratulations, they were telling each other how awful I looked.

Fortunately, before I could really lose my temper, Mum turned her back on Nonna and Dad. Giving me her special smile, the one which meant her and me against the world, she said in English, 'I think Mia looks wonderful!' And ignoring Dad's cross expression and Nonna's angry muttering, she said, 'Mia looks so good, tomorrow we'll go shopping for new clothes.'

While the others frowned in disapproval, Mum and I beamed happily at each other.

The rest of the holidays disappeared very

rapidly. Determined not to waste all the money and effort I'd put into losing so much weight, I kept to my new eating style, in spite of everything Nonna and Dad said. Mum, on the other hand, was so impressed, she immediately joined my new way of eating.

My first afternoon home she got me to describe it. 'Anything that's low in fat and sugar is fine,' I explained. 'The idea is you fill up on fruit, grain and vegies, cut back on meat, cheese and refined carbohydrates.'

'Right!' she said, all enthusiastic. But a bit later on I caught her tasting Nonna's special cheese-cake — the one with threads of dark chocolate running through the top. She jumped when she saw me watching, then guiltily explained, 'Just testing that the standard's up to the usual.'

'Lucky I'm not Dr Drabble,' I said, 'or you'd be out of here in a flash.'

Of course, mentioning Dr Drabble reminded me of Kirsty, and everything that had happened.

I went to the phone and dialed her number. A lady's voice answered. She introduced herself as Kirsty's mum. 'Kirsty's in hospital. She's not on the phone but I'll give her your message.'

'Give her my love. Tell her I'm thinking about her ...' My voice trailed away. How could I tell Kirsty how worried I was about her and Rebecca? But Kirsty's mum knew what I was thinking. 'I certainly will. You must be worried.'

'I am.' I cleared my throat. 'I mean, I was. How's she getting on?'

'Fine.' She sounded like she meant it. 'She'll be out in a couple of weeks. I'll get her to ring you tomorrow.'

Next day, when Kirsty rang, I asked. 'What's the hospital like?'

'Rough!' Her laugh reminded me how much I was missing her already. 'They're talking about putting staples in my stomach. They'd have done it already, only Mum says I'm too young.'

'Staples in your stomach? Sounds drastic. Isn't there something else they can do?'

'No, not a thing. It's like they said in camp: The buck stops with you.' Another laugh.

'How's Rebecca?'

Kirsty's voice turned serious. 'A bit better. At least she's stopped losing weight.'

'That's good!' I wished I could think of something to say that showed how much I missed them already, 'You'll give her my love?'

'Of course. And I'll ring again. Maybe next week?'

'Terrific,' I said. And she rang off.

After I put down the phone, I felt really depressed. I'd never realised before how quickly you could get attached to new friends. I was already missing Kirsty, missing her intelligent mind and amazing laugh. And I fretted about her and Rebecca, and about their awful diseases.

Over the next month, Kirsty phoned me at least twice a week. That gave me another, more secret problem. Basically it was that each time I spoke to Kirsty, I'd brood even more about Con. And the more I brooded over Con, the more convinced I was that I'd treated him really badly. Come to think of it, I'd treated him almost as badly as Gerard used to treat Soula. I'd never blame Con if he didn't ever want to speak to me again. But each time I told myself this, I'd just feel worse.

The only positive in my life — apart from

giving Mum a well deserved break from the Pizzeria and working with Dad where I was learning heaps about the hospitality business — was making sure I kept up some kind of physical activity.

I was lucky that Dad didn't open up until noon. This meant I could spend my mornings however I liked. So I'd be off first thing, running the three kilometres to our local swimming pool. There, after stripping to my bathers (I always wore them under my jogging shorts) I'd try and swim twenty laps. Early on, still exhausted by so much exercising, I'd tram back home. But later, once I got stronger I always walked.

I've always loved swimming. There's something about ploughing through the water, the rhythmical movement of your arms and legs, the steady, even breathing that blocks out every other thought.

Though I used to be a really good swimmer, I lost interest when I reached my teens. I remember telling everyone I didn't like stripping off, hated jumping into cold water, loathed the smell of chlorine. 'Anyway,' I'd add. 'It's a real pest having to shampoo your hair.' The real reason was because I was scared someone would see me in bathers, see how fat I was.

But now, with all my newfound knowledge about exercise, plus my different way of eating, things had certainly changed. After climbing out of the pool — and after my heart stopped pounding, my shoulders, arms and legs stopped aching and I'd shaken the water out of my ears so I could hear once again — I'd feel so good, so buoyant, I could hardly believe it.

This complicated routine took up most of my morning, but as long as I got up early enough, it fitted neatly into the Pizzeria's hours. Though I was only managing six or maybe seven hours sleep, the more energy I used, the more I seemed to find. By the end of the third week, I was running home from the pool, ready to burst out of my skin, I was feeling so great.

And there were other unexpected bonuses. My eyes had never looked as clear, my skin as good, or my hair as glossy. Mum said I looked like a slinky jungle cat.

But I wasn't seeing much of Soula. She was

spending her holidays in the sandwich shop helping her mum. And with *her* hours being six a.m. to four, and *mine* being noon to midnight, though we faithfully phoned each other at least three times a week, we never met more than once a fortnight.

Meanwhile she and Ben stayed close. Though I was really pleased for her, at the same time I couldn't help feeling left out. Not that she'd dumped me or anything, but it was hard being on my own. I told myself I'd been too dependent on Soula, too used to doing everything together. Once I had less to do, I promised myself, I'd expand my circle of friends, get to know more people. Maybe I'd even join a sporting club. Take up netball and squash.

Only later. Later, when I had heaps more time. Right now I was having enough trouble getting through everything else to worry about my non-existent social life.

So in one way, the rest of the holidays were a drag. But in another — working in the Pizzeria, learning heaps about catering, keeping up with my exercise routine and finishing my reading for

Year 12 — they disappeared in a puff of smoke.

But all my efforts were paying off. By the end of January, by the time I was ready to report back to Donyvale, I had lost the last six kilos and, out of my own money, bought myself a fantastic wardrobe.

Actually, I was getting pretty vain. For the first time ever, I enjoyed seeing myself in the mirror. One thing led to another. I spent some of my hard earned cash on a new hairstyle.

When I got home, Mum made a big fuss of how good I looked. In the bathroom, I examined myself from every angle. For once I was pleasantly surprised. The reflection showed a slim, good-looking girl, with beautiful hair, who looked ready to take on the world.

Failing the world, I told myself, I was certainly ready to take on Guy Prescott *and* the rest of Year 12.

Chapter 16

Day one of term one, for once we got to school on time. Soula yawned hugely; 'Only because you got me up so early!'

'Got to get in that early morning run!' I jogged on the spot.

Right then we were in the Girls, on our way to our first Year 12 Assembly. First checking that my new jeans, white T-shirt and Reeboks weren't getting crumpled or dirty, I pulled out a brush and started work on my hair.

Soula was inspecting herself in the mirror. She looked terrific. I asked, 'You lost any more weight?'

'Some,' she nodded. 'Only not as much as you.'

I tried viewing her through a stranger's eyes. Maybe I was biased, but the final effect was still stunning. Now Soula's face was no longer puffy, you could see those high cheekbones, that beautiful curly hair which surged down her back like it had life of its own.

And like me, she'd spent the previous week shopping, spending most of her summer earnings on some great new clothes. Now we were perfect size 10s, buying clothes was a dream. At the moment we were both so addicted to shopping, we could barely drag ourselves away from department stores and shopping malls. To tell the truth, I'd bought so many new clothes, my wardrobe was about to burst. I couldn't fit another thing in.

Mum didn't mind. 'After all, dear,' she said to me. 'You earned the money, so you get to spend it any way you choose.'

If Dad worried, I never knew. Even if he didn't like me spending so much, he never said anything.

Only Nonna disapproved. 'You should be saving for when you start university,' she said in Italian. 'What will happen to all these clothes when you're back to your proper size? Anyway, aren't you tired of all this shopping?'

'No,' I said. I certainly wasn't. 'Besides, Nonna, I'm my proper size right now.'

She pressed her lips into that expression which I knew meant she disagreed. Only this time I refused to get drawn into any of our old arguments.

Maybe it *was* just a phase on my part, but I figured it was going to take me a long, long time to get frustrated, bored or sick of buying clothes.

Just as I was thinking this, the door flew open and Karinna, Joanne and Tara came barging in.

They stared at us in surprise. 'Hello! Who are you?'

We slowly turned round.

Watching their confusion and recognition — not to mention how pissed-off they looked — I wished I'd thought of bringing a camera to record their shocked faces.

And did Soula and I enjoy every single second

of it?

You bet we did.

After all, didn't we deserve it? Wasn't this one of the moments we'd both been working for?

But instead of hanging around to listen to the inevitable 'oohs' and 'ahs', and answering questions on how we'd managed to lose so much weight, Soula and I grabbed our stuff, sailed out the door, down the corridor and into the Year 12 Common Room.

A football sailed past me and bounded into the corridor. Soula lunged, caught it and tossed it to Gerard. Sam Holdsworthy jumped in front and he and Gerard went crashing onto the floor.

'What ...!' I looked up. Mr Hesketh was standing there, his face bright red. 'What on earth?' His roar could be heard at the other end of the building. 'Everyone sit down!'

Everyone did.

Mr Hesketh glared angrily around, then pointed at Soula and me. 'Is this how Year 12 students behave in front of new students?'

Someone whistled loudly.

'Hey ... girls ...!'

'They're not new …'

'Good God! It's Soula and Mia!'

'Wow!'

Then another loud whistle.

The door burst open once again. This time Guy stormed in. Catching sight of us, his mouth dropped open in disbelief.

At least Guy doesn't have to be introduced all over again, I thought, watching him head straight for me. It was pretty obvious just from the gleam in his eyes that he liked … he *really* liked … what he was seeing.

Later on that day … much, much later, we were all sitting in one of our local cafes, sipping cappuccinos. Well, the others were sipping cappuccinos. Soula and me were drinking mineral water. Everyone knows that mineral water is much better for you than coffee.

We'd already been there a fair while when Soula looked at her watch, then whispered, 'Gotta go. I promised Ben I'd see him at five.'

Meanwhile Gerard was carrying on like an idiot. Watching him balance a cup on his forehead — he kept fumbling and dropping it, watching the way he tried to get Soula's attention — ignoring Tara who was getting madder by the minute, I had to remind myself this was the same guy Soula had once so hopelessly adored.

What a nerd he was. Remembering how he used to con Soula to finish off his maths assignments and his biology pracs, act like his slave, I could hardly believe the same person was sitting opposite me. Back then Soula would pretend not to mind too much when Gerard refused to talk to her in public. How things had changed. Now she was treating him like he was a bad case of hepatitis. What's more, I knew for a fact she really meant it.

I don't like sounding bitchy, but I couldn't help enjoying it all. No matter how hard I tried, I couldn't come up with one other person who deserved that kind of treatment as much as Gerard Moloney.

Just as I was thinking how lucky I was to be keen on Guy — I mean, though he's Gerard's best friend he isn't like him at all — a sudden movement brought me back to earth.

Guy was handing me yet another bottle of mineral water, paid for by him. Shoving Karinna out of the way, he settled beside me.

'Those idiots have just run out of your brand.' He sounded as if he'd never forgive the management for making such a terrible mistake. But there was something more important he wanted to say. 'Mia ...' those baby blues gazed deep into mine, 'You going to Joanne's party?'

I blinked. 'Joanne's party? Actually ... I hadn't given it much thought.'

I was lying through my teeth. For the last couple of days I hadn't thought about much else. If only Guy asks me to that party, I'd prayed. And now my dreams were coming true ...

Savouring the moment, like you'd savour a forbidden Mars Bar or a Cherry Ripe, I held my breath. Eventually Guy got around to saying, 'You wouldn't think of coming with me, would you?'

Slowly — very, very slowly — I pretended to consider his offer. 'I guess that'd be okay.'

I was so determined to keep my delight from showing, I only half took in Karinna. Seated opposite, her mouth was twisted into a jealous line. She was watching every move Guy made. Turning to Tara, she said, 'I've just met this great new guy!'

And making sure no one in the cafe could miss hearing her voice, 'I'm bringing him to Joanne's party. Just wait till you meet him!'

Chapter 17

Looking back, maybe what I wore to the party *was* a bit much.

Though Nonna's lips tightened disapprovingly, all she said was, 'It's cool out there. Take a jacket.'

The two of us stared at my reflection. I was wearing a strapless dark green velvet bodice with gold beading, a very short swishy skirt in the same green, and matching shoes. My eyeliner was dark green and so was my eyeshadow. That particular shade, the same colour as my eyes, made my skin seem paler and brought out the red in my hair. And though the outfit, including the make-up had cost me a queen's ransom, the total effect was terrific.

Guy seemed to think so too, because when I opened the door, his eyes practically popped out of his head. 'Mia! You look fantastic!'

In a dinner jacket, high white collar, black tie and embroidered shirt, I thought he looked pretty cool himself. But instead of saying something nice in return, I just smiled, and with my feet barely touching the ground, sailed out our front door. The last thing I wanted was for Guy to know how inexperienced I was. I told myself I'd die if he ever guessed this was my first proper date.

Guy had brought his dad's car. Careful not to crush my skirt, I climbed inside. He made a point of opening then shutting the door behind me. Then, all without speaking, he hopped into the driver's seat, roared down the road, did a right hand turn into Patterson Street, and squealed to a stop in front of Joanne's house.

The entire neighbourhood must've know there was a party on, because the amplifiers were turned up as high as they would go.

Guy and I were late. Without even bothering to see who else was there, just calling 'Hi, you two,' to Gerard and Tara as they danced by, he grabbed me round the waist and we started dancing too. The song was a slow, slinky, sexy one. And while we danced, Guy kept pressing against me, and touching me. It was the moment I'd waited for, I guess.

But why did he have to be so obvious?

Just then Soula and Ben danced by. When they saw what was going on, they gave us with that look people get when they think you're acting too gross for words.Guy was so blatant about what he planned to do later on, once we were alone, it was like he was announcing to the whole world I was his property. Even so, I didn't do anything to stop him.

I mean, wasn't this the attention I'd been waiting for all these years?

But Guy wasn't even bothering to talk to me. It was almost as if now, now at long last he'd got interested in me as a sex object, that was *all* I was.

Then I noticed he'd edged me to the door and

into the hallway. Shoving our way through the crowd, I heard a loud voice, then caught sight of Karinna. Someone very familiar was standing next to her, smiling at Soula and Ben.

Con!

Con was here. Con was here with Karinna...

What on earth was Con doing with Karinna?

Jealousy hit me like a bomb.

There was just time to note how great he looked before Guy was pulling me through the doorway, saying, 'Come on, Mia. Stop wasting time.'

Right then Con caught sight of me.

The moment our eyes met, I knew who it was I really wanted.

I wanted Con.

Like in slow motion, I had time to notice his startled face, and then his smile... Hey, Con was happy to see me! Then I saw him take in what was happening.

Like I'd turned into a fly on the wall, I watched Guy pull me through the doorway.

Too late.

The coldness of Con's look seemed to paralyse

me. I let Guy drag me outside, and then the fresh air hit me like a bucket of water.

Guy was pulling me to the car. He unlocked the door...was pushing me inside...

Who was this guy, anyway? Who *was* Guy Prescott? I suddenly realised I didn't really know him.

What's more, I didn't really like him.

I edged away. 'Guy. Please don't do that...!'

'Huh?' Guy paused, then continued his assault.

A good thing I was fit. Reaching out, I shoved him away. I was stronger than I realised, and his head hit the window.

'Ouch!'

My shove really hurt. He stopped wrestling me long enough to rub his head, and I grabbed the door handle, pushed open the door and rushed outside.

There didn't seem much point going back inside. I readjusted my clothes and headed straight home.

'I keep trying to get over Con,' I moaned. 'But it

just won't work.'

This time Kirsty didn't laugh. Instead of saying that it served me right, and it was my own stupid fault, she patted my arm. 'Rebecca and me, we're thinking. We're thinking.'

I managed a smile. 'I came to see how *you* two were. I mean, I shouldn't be bothering you with my problems. It's not as if you haven't got enough of your own.'

'Nothing that isn't self-inflicted,' Rebecca answered.

'That's not true!'

'Isn't it?' Rebecca's eyes met mine. 'Didn't the doctors promise we'd be out of here in a couple of weeks if we behaved? It's not their fault it took us ages to sort ourselves out.'

'It could've been worse. I can hardly believe you're both so much better.'

They grinned at each other. Now that their weird eating patterns were more or less under control, Kirsty was visibly thinner and Rebecca actually looked like a human being. Both of them looked so much better, I could hardly believe it.

'Anyway,' Kirsty waved her arm. 'It's not as if

this place is so bad. It's not like living in a hospital, is it?'

'It's much nicer than I expected.' I said, looking around. There were prints on the walls, the beds were separated by brightly covered screens and covered in handmade quilts, there were two television sets and video recorders, a C.D. and tape player, and the shelves were filled with interesting looking books.

'Now, Mia,' said Kirsty. 'We're getting away from the subject. Which is...'

'...what she has to do to get Con interested in her again,' Rebecca added.

'No.' I shook my head. 'It's hopeless. I reckon I've stuffed it. I shouldn't have gone home early. Now Con thinks I spent the night having sex with Guy. Karinna's bound to tell him I did, anyway.'

Rebecca frowned. 'What's to say he'll believe her?'

'What's to say he'd care?' I sighed. 'Especially if he likes Karinna enough to take her out. How'd she get to meet him, anyway?'

Kirsty laughed. 'Haven't you heard? He got

a job cleaning Karinna's mother's house, so Karinna asked him to the party. But Con's no dummy. You've said so yourself. Karinna sounds gross. Maybe he'll figure her out for himself?'

Rebecca looked doubtful. 'But what if he doesn't? Let's face it, Con never tells anyone what's going on in his mind.'

I stared through the window to where the trees were beginning to droop. They certainly matched my mood. If only there was some way of getting Con interested in me again.

'No,' I said at last. 'Con certainly doesn't tell anyone what he's thinking.'

We looked at each other and shrugged.

Chapter 18

Autumn brought grey skies, squally rainstorms and an icy wind that tore through your clothes, leaving you cold and hungry.

The next couple of weeks I got really low. Because I was feeling low, I stopped swimming. My eating patterns changed. That empty feeling returned. It was the kind of empty feeling that could only be filled with hamburgers and milkshakes, chips and pizza, Cherry Ripes, Mars Bars, and Tim Tams.

No Guy to dream about any more. No Con

to make me feel better. If Con were around he'd make me feel heaps better. No Con. No nothing. Nothing. A fat lot of difference losing all that weight had down to my life.

'Now listen, Mia, you've got to make an effort to snap out of it,' Soula said. 'You're not doing yourself any favours, are you?'

'No!' I said, eyeing off the fresh packet of Tim Tams on the table beside me.

I shifted the phone to my other ear. Soula's voice got louder. 'Fancy putting on three kilos. No wonder you're depressed. You'll be back to your old weight in no time flat. What you need is to start swimming again. Watch what you're eating...'

'Yes.' I edged the packet closer.

'Anyway...' she was saying, 'What are you doing tomorrow night? Me and Ben want to take you to this new disco. We'll pick you up at eight.'

'Huh?' I thought wildly. 'But I haven't got anything to wear...'

'You'll find something. Be ready on time.'

'But...'

Before I could think of a decent excuse, she'd

slammed down the phone.

Saturday morning Mum woke up with the flu, so it was left to me to help Dad out. With one thing and another, I didn't get home until well after seven. That left exactly forty minutes to wade through my wardrobe, find something to wear, then shower and change.

I stared at my clothes in disgust. Hopeless. Everything was hopeless. In the end I settled for an old pair of jeans, a sloppy T-shirt and an all-covering jacket. Back to my old ways of dressing. Back to my old dreary ways. I could hardly even be bothered fixing my hair and face.

Ben and Soula turned up on the dot of eight.

I stared at them. They looked terrific. They were slim and gorgeous. I hated them both. It was the first time I'd ever felt envy towards my closest friend.

But if they thought I was looking fat and horrible, they were tactful enough not to say so.

'Come on, we're late.'

They walked me out to where Ben had parked his car. Though it was dark, I could see someone sitting in the rear.

Something about the guy's shape was familiar. My heart nearly stopped.

Con! Was that really Con?

Petrified, I stopped walking and stared at the car. Right now, now that I was back to being fat, Con was the last person I wanted to see. What would he think when he saw me properly? Surely he'd despise me for putting on all that weight?

Before I could rush back inside the house, Soula was pushing me into the rear. I sat down next to him. When I did manage to look up, he was smiling at me like he was really pleased I was there. 'Mia. Great to see you.'

'Hi, Con.'

As Ben drove us to the disco, while he and Soula kept up a steady stream of conversation from the front, things felt awkward between us.

All these thoughts kept churning round and round in my brain. There was so much to say, yet so much I didn't dare mention. I wasn't sure of Con's reaction to being with me, or even mine to being with him. Like it was all happening in a dream, I answered politely when anyone spoke to me, and the rest of the time I stayed silent. While Soula and Ben chattered away about school and uni, Con was his usual quiet self. Anytime I caught his eye, he smiled like he was happy to see me. To be with me. It suddenly struck me Con was acting like he was still interested.

How was this possible? Wasn't he interested in Karinna? And anyway, who'd like someone as fat and unattractive as me? To tell the truth, I didn't know what to think.

I spent most of that night in a daze. I remember we danced together while the music was playing. And when it stopped Con bought me a drink, then walked me outside. We didn't talk much, but when we did we didn't talk about ourselves. For once *he* did most of the talking. He talked about the people we knew from Camp.

But it wasn't until he mentioned Kirsty and Rebecca and we realised we'd both been to visit them in hospital that the tension started melting away.

'They're feeling much better,' I told him. 'And

they're really grateful for everything you did.'

'It was nothing!' I could tell he was embarrassed.

Another long pause. There was so much I wanted to say, but I kept wondering how to say it.

Then we both started talking at once:

'Con, I think you were terrific to Kirsty and Rebecca...'

'Mia, my feelings for you haven't changed...'

We looked at each other and laughed.

'My turn first,' Con said. 'I want you to know that I didn't contact you because Karinna told me you were still going out with Guy.'

I shook my head, too shy and embarrassed to look him straight in the eye.

'But the other day, when I went to visit Kirsty, she hinted how you really felt. At first I didn't believe her. So I went and checked with Soula.' He paused for a moment. 'Were they telling the truth?'

'Yes,' I whispered.

He stared at me. 'So why didn't you contact me?'

'I didn't think you'd be interested. You see, I'd put on all this weight...'

'You think a few extra kilos makes a difference to how I feel?' I'd never heard him sound so angry. 'Don't you think I like you for all sorts of other reasons? And just in case you're not sure, I'll spell them out...'

Putting his arms around me, he whispered in my ear, and the list was pretty convincing.

Then he bent over and kissed me.

Con may not look like he just stepped out of a Country Road catalogue — but by now I knew better than anyone that a great relationship depends on much more than that. Thank goodness.

FREE SEND-AWAY MAKE-UP OFFER

To celebrate the launch of this brilliant new series, Lovelines are offering a FREE matching Boots 17 Pure Colour Lipstick and Nail Polish with every two books purchased.

To claim your free gift, simply collect till receipts for two books and send them with the coupon below to: Lovelines/17 Make Up Offer, Pan Macmillan Children's Books, 18-21 Cavaye Place, London SW10 9PG

Terms and Conditions: Offer ends 31st December 1993. All free gifts will be dispatched within 28 days. There is no cash alternative. Free gifts will not be dispatched without proof of purchase. Offer limited to one free gift per person.

✂···

Name _____

Address _____

_____

Age _____

I wish to claim my free 17 lip and nail gift for buying the following titles (please list):

1. _____

2. _____

PAN